The Eminent Souls

The Eminent Souls

History Rewinds

SATYAM NANDA

PARTRIDGE
A Penguin Random House Company

ISBN: Softcover 978-1-4828-4347-7
eBook 978-1-4828-4346-0

This book is a complete work of fiction. Any resemblance to living or dead is purely coincidental. All the names and characters are fictional. Some famous names are used to give a background to the story but they have no link with real facts of history. There is no intention to hurt the sentiments of any individual, community, section or religion.

To order additional copies of this book, contact
Partridge India
000 800 10062 62
orders.india@partridgepublishing.com

www.partridgepublishing.com/india

CONTENTS

'Dedicated to my
dear Brother.
Anything Sweeter
than you is yet to be
discovered.'

CH - 1

The start of the voyage

Hundreds of thunders, and clouds clashing in the sky. Looks like announcing the onset of a STROM. And clouds entirely overpowering the sun. Therefore, when ample are already awake, the clock showing 6 of the dawn, feels like it's still night.

And finally... it has started raining... raining heavily. And so the lonely long street in the European market looks lonelier and more horrible.

In the center of the street is a diminutive old rest house. Inside is sitting an old ugly pale man with glowing sapphire eyes, staring at the cloudburst outside. He is holding a hot cup in one hand with a cigar in between the middle fingers and a newspaper in other. The newspaper reads the date of the day... '5 October 1939, 'European Times' London.

And there is a colossal brown dog sitting quietly besides the elderly man. It's hard to tell who is more ugly, the dog or the master.

And from the stairs besides, descends a man with a brown repugnant coat, dark brown pants and a loose tie. He is brown, an 'INDIAN'. The young man asked the rent from the hideous looking receptionist.

The old man gives him a pen and points towards the register that was kept on the table. After filling the information, he takes out money from his pocket and hand it over to the man. H7e takes his hat and the over coat to proceed.

The register reads-
Name of the customer -_Amar_
No. of days stayed - _1_

While smoking the old white man interrupted "Hey young man...... It's raining, and my experience says it will go better and better." He gives him umbrella and adds "You will need it."

Passing an innocent smile Amar takes the umbrella "Thanks for the umbrella BUT...... you shouldn't smoke, it's not good for health."

And he opens the door, comes out and gathers courage to face the rain.

As the door closes leisurely, another dog comes outside with his one leg broken, trying to be faster than the door. Most probably he is with Amar.

The ugly one barks at him. And the cute white creature slightly frightened but tries to be tougher, creeps outside, making a near escape to save his tiny tail.

"Oh, so you are also ready? ...... Scott" said Amar. "I thought you would like to stay back. How is your leg now?"

"Let's go dad" shockingly the dog replies. Scott, the dog tries to communicate to others but fails, as it always sound like a dog's bark.

He barks and wave his tale, and Amar takes him in his lap as he know that Scott hate rains and rainy roads.
Both start their journey and soon they disappear in the heavy dense rain......

CH - 2

A pinch of science

"The shower has turned into a tempest (peeping out of the window) now what about clothes" says the pleasantly plump owner of 'SAM DRYCLEANER STORE'. The weather has gone unnatural and the clouds are thundering like never before.

"Don't worry Boss, I have arranged a horse cart" replies his employ busy ironing the white bed sheets.

Sam Murphy, the owner of the primeval drycleaner goes towards his cubbyhole and opens it. He takes out an umbrella and as he moves to go outside, out of the blue Scott hops on the spot and barks on him heavily.

Sam screams out of fright "Aaaa.... Shoo shooo"

Amar enters the scene and orders Scott to shut.

"Take him away" said Sam.

"I am sorry sir".

"Leave it, why are you late?"

"Rain Mr. Murphy..."

"First Day of the job and here comes the first excuse... this thing don't work in Sam's Store, ask him" Pointing towards the other employ ironing the clothes, "I told you that I am the only drycleaner in the vicinity who clean the clothes for the Officers and the elite class. They simply don't give the clothes to anyone else, because they only rely on me and my work" Amar takes a long breath "That's why I have a 2 year contract with the public departments and their officers"

The other employ interrupts "Sir... your coffee would be ready till now"

"Ahh... coffee" gazing at Amar "You wait for me here". Amar bowed his head in approval while Sam left the place.

"I got it that he has started again" said the other employ "You are new here?"

"Yes"

"Hi, I am David" approaching towards his hands.

"Amar"

"We should leave, it's already 9:30, keep these clothes in that cart outside"

Amar kept the bunch of clothes in the cart and both of them sat inside it. Scott came by escaping from the horse's leg and start gawking at Amar.

"What?" asks Amar, "Stay here today, your leg wouldn't be fully fine. I will take you tomorrow...

Scott turned and went inside the store murmuring "If you don't know what lack of attention is, then become a dog." The horses move on, taking the cart far from the sight.

The cart stops in front of a big mansion. Both of them enter the house holding white sheets and clothes in their hands. A policeman stops them at the door, David showed him a piece of paper and enter inside.

Amar asks inquisitively "What was it".

"A written approval, you can't enter such a big scientist's house just like a housefly. He is Elbert Einstein brother, father of the scientists."

"Yes he is" staring towards the stairs going upwards.

David murmurs "They said that he has a lab there upstairs"

"Leave the clothes and leave" shouted the policeman.

"I have to take back some clothes too, I am waiting for the maid" David shouts back.

"Hey.... David, I will take the clothes from the maid, I think if we are going to wait for her than the other deliveries will get delayed"

"Perfect. Okay then, meet you at the store"

"Bye"

They shake hands and David leaves the room. Amar put forth his steps towards the stairs when abruptly the maid interrupts him "Where are you going?"

Amar takes out a card out of his jacket "I am from the Queen's Office, is Sir here?"

The maid stares at him for some time, "sir you please wait upstairs, he must be busy in the attic."

He climbs the stairs and notices fruits and deserts decorated on a plate. The maid climbs up the stairs and saw him starring towards her, and goes towards the attic. She opened the door and in a corner a man with grey hairs was busy noting something on a paper.

"Sir...... Sir"

And the greatest scientist ever, Albert Einstein, turned his neck, the man with the grey hair. "Yes"

"Sir, a gentleman is waiting for you downstairs, someone from the Queens Office"

"Tell him I am busy, I am not meeting anyone today, the Queen can wait"

"Ok Sir.... And your breakfast is also ready"

"I will have it, thanks"

At the other side Amar was fighting with his hunger, and when finally he failed, he goes near to the table and got scared when someone hold him from his back.

"He has cancelled all the meetings, he said he is not going to meet anyone today" says the maid in a monotonous tone.

"But tell him I am from the Queens office"

"He said the Queen can wait"

"Queen can wait? Its urgent, let me...."

"I am sorry sir" and the door bell rang "Excuse me Sir". And she leaves.

He turns around and starts bowling the food inside his belly like a ravenous animal, leaving a messy table. The wooden stairs started creating noises which give him an indication that someone is descending down. He swiftly hides behind the curtains.

Mr. Albert Einstein watches the table messy and the plates empty, and murmurs "Plates are empty, may be... I have eaten the breakfast and forgotten" He turns to climb up the attic, and Amar also takes out his foot to escape when suddenly a new voice enters the atmosphere.

"Sir"

The scientist descends the two stairs he had climbed "Oh! Sophie, Good morning my child"

"Good morning sir" replied the scientist's young secretary. Amar took out his eyes but couldn't see the girl, who was standing by facing her back towards him." You are coming to the Research Center tomorrow for signing the documents."

"I will try, not feeling like going anywhere, someone from the queen's office came to meet me", Sophie turned her neck to see the person her eyes had missed, "Who?"

Amar hides behind the curtains again.

"I don't know may be he has gone". The scientist replies.

"I will get the paper ready, ok I should take your leave"

"Meet you tomorrow darling". And he climbs up the stairs.

The girl descends down and went outside, Amar came out of his refuge and ran towards the exit to follow the girl. Suddenly the policeman interrupts him and says "Hey you washerman, what are you doing here, leave now or...."

"I am leaving" He angrily replied

CH - 3

The girl in the office

The next day, Amar and Scott left the rest house in the crack of dawn. It has been two days since it's raining so heavily.

Covering quite a dripping distance, they came to a mammoth building –'THE SCIENCE and RESEARCH CENTRE'. Big eyes of the young guy showing his life-size dreams confirms that the destination has come.

Seeing the board that conveys 'DOGS not allowed', Scott starts barking "Oh no, Not again." And he jumps out of his lap as if he knows what to do at the times when he has to face such sign boards.

"Hey Mickey Mouse, stay here and don't go anywhere chasing the bitches" shouts Amar.

"I don't promise dad" and he sits under the shelter.

Amar enters inside and starts folding his umbrella, out of the blue his eyes plunges on a gorgeous young girl, sitting on front table, and the umbrella slips through his hand and opens with a thraaaassssshhhhh......

The sudden noise makes even the busiest one in the office to ogle at the Indian lad. But he is looking like a lost man. He has gone yellow and is stunned. With gazing eyes, he puts forth his step towards the girl...

"Oh my God, what the hell are you doing here?" screams Amar

The girl asks "Sorry sir, may I help you?"

He yells "Keep your help with you Meghana, and don't try to make a fool out of me. Ho...Ho...How do you come here, what was the need to come? I had told you that I will come back soon".

She replies surprisingly "Please sir, I think you have been mistaken, my name is Sophie and please don't shout, it's an office".

Amar angrily throws an ink pot on the floor "Now what do you want me to do?".

"Now, enough... enough. You are crossing all the limits. Please get out".

"I will kill you".

"Security...security......"

Amar gets heated up "What? I can't believe it's you".

"That's the same thing I am saying," she tries to cool up the air "you are misunderstanding. I am not that whom you are finding for".

A Police Officer runs towards the hot spot. "Yes madam".

"Officer Clark, Please throw this gentleman out" requests Sophie.

Amar holds Officer Clark's from his collar and shouts "Oh my God, Munish, first tell me, now what new games you're playing? How the hell you came here bastard?"

All the security men and policemen come to the rescue of Officer Clark and chucks Amar away.

Unwrinkeling his shirt Officer Clark commanded "Arrest this man". The policemen make him lie on the floor and tie his hands from his back.

"Leave me you bastards." Amar shouts "And I will see you Munish, you bloody..."
"Take this man in custody" Officer Clark orders.

Sophie smiles "Thank you Officer"
"It's my duty madam. But you have to do a favor".

"F..f favor......" she gets tensed, gives a thought and smiles "Oh... I am sorry. I am on diet so I don't drink coffee these days".

"Oh no, you are misinterpreting me lady. I mean you have to come to the Police Station for registering a report against this man".

She gets mortified "Oh sorry, I…I I will, I will".

As the policemen comes out holding Amar along, Scott starts barking knowingly that whatever happened inside was not good for his master. "Leave my dad, you bastards" he barks.

"Shut up you dirty creature" Officer shouts "and take this Mickey Mouse to the Police station".
And as he proceeds

"You Bloody Dog……" and Scott bites hard on officer's butt.

Officer starts screaming but the so called dirty creature is unwilling to leave.

Now Amar commanded the policemen with poise… "Go go… save your Officer, hahaha… I am not going to run".

Now it was a site to be must watched, as Scott biting the officer's butt and 4-5 policemen pulling him away.

Officer "Aaah… take this awful thing away Aaah…"

Amar laughs "Pull him away… Pull him away... hahaha……"

And as they pull, Scott also gets along a big piece of officer's pant and boxers …

Even the policemen can't stop themselves to share a laugh.

Officer howls due to the twinge "Huuuh, ooo aaah..." and shouts "shut up... shut up......"

Making his chest broader "I am sorry for the pant Officer, and yes, please bear in mind to get injected, Hahaha...." scheming his laughter "Sorry again..."

Officer tries to cover his torn pants "You...... aaah... take him to the Police station".

Policeman pushes him "Move...".

"Hey I have left my umbrella inside, just wait," Amar cries "I have to give it back to someone, it's not mine." Policemen pull him towards the police car "Are you all deaf?" The car starts moving "Hey... my umbrella......"

CH - 4

Regrettable imprisonment

"Dad... Dad......"

It's 5 of the evening and it's still raining, and the poor Scott, despite hating the shower, is crying for his master while sitting in front of the old building with the umbrella under his feet which his master forgot.

The building is most probably the Police Station where his master had been arrested.

He barks and barks, hoping that Amar would listen.

Amar sitting inside the cell realizes that his sincere dog is waiting for him and the pending lunch.

He feels sorry for the pretty white creature, and suddenly a policeman hop and bang the bars of the cell with his rod.

"Hey Mickey Mouse, come out. You have been called". He comes out and starts walking at the snail's pace.

"Move fast".

Amar replied rudely "After so much torture, you expect me to move fast, I can't".

They reach the office where the Officer and Sophie were sitting.

"Hey, leave me for a minute." He shakes his hand and asks the officer "Can I get my hat?"

Officer orders the policeman "Give him his hat."

"Yes sir" and the policeman goes outside the room.

Amar goes towards Sophie and sits on his knees "A.a..a… are you sure, th..that you have never seen me before?"

Sophie crouches her eyes and shakes her head in rejection.

The policeman enters the room and gives him the hat "Take it".

Holding the hat "Thanks" he turns towards Sophie and asks her graciously "A. a.. a...and what's your name?"

"Sophie"

"So...... Miss... Sophie, I am very sorry. You resemble my friend. I...I am really feeling guilty. I am in a problem. Please...please"

Officer Clark interrupts "Ok I agree, then what about me".

"You resemble one of my friend. Sorry sir, today's day is really very unlucky. I am in a hurry, please leave me".

Officer Puts a cigarette in his mouth "Then first tell me, how many friends you have, so that we could save the other look alikes".

Amar took the cigarette out of the officer's mouth and throws it. "Sorry sir, I have problem with the smoke" Officer stares at him with cunning eyes, "and moreover it's also bad for your health, you should leave it...... I mean I...I ponder the whole day while the policemen were beating brutally, that...that I have created a big blunder".

Sophie pleads "Please officer, I think it's a matter of misunderstanding, I sense like, this person is innocent".

Officer replies monotonously "That is totally our work madam to find who is innocent and who is not".

Sophie interrupts "Sir, I promise there will be no further dispute".

"Really?" Amar stares towards Sophie "I mean if she's saying so then it would..."

Officer Clark interrupts "Hmmm... ok madam "he warns Amar "but behave yourself, next time it will be the last one".

Amar nodded his head with bowed eyes.

Officer annoyingly says "Now get lost".

Amar and Sophie both come out together and suddenly Scott comes running "Dad... Dad......"

Sophie got frightened and holds Amar tightly. "Shoo shooo......"

Amar bend on his knees to greet his dog. Scott jumps on his knees.

"Don't worry, he doesn't harm."

Sophie shouts alarmingly "If that so, then what was that which I saw in the morning."

"Oh, that's an exception, Scott hate policemen, but he loves sweet girls and me too."

"And what else you like?"

"Coffee...... You?"

"Ok".

CH - 5

The so called first date

Both were sitting on the opposite chairs at a coffee shop, with each cup of coffee and absolute silence......

The motionless environment was jampacked with bashfulness and loads of unanswered questions.

Amar breaks the stillness "So...... are you married?"

Sophie shook her head in a timid no.

"Ok...... "Feeling like he shouldn't inquire
"You?"

"No, I am also single. In fact I am thinking of getting married soon."

Sophie passes a bashful smile.

"And... you are a receptionist?"

"No, I am personal secretary to the head of the research centre. You know who is he?" and her eyes glitters.

"Yes......" pressing his tooth.
"And you, you are a tourist?" she asks

"Can you help me?"

"Of course".

"I want to meet Mr. Elbert Einstein......"

Silence again conquer the environment
"I got it" Sophie replies with a heated look, "this all presentation was to impress me, you want to use me as a link to the head, am I right?"

"No, completely no dear, our first encounter was just a coincidence".

After having a thought "ummm...... but, no, it's not possible, you can't meet him".
"But why?"
"You don't know, its World War II, and Mr. Elbert Einstein is the main head for research and science against soviet group".

"But you are her personal secretary".
"I am just a helper".
"But you can do it, it's really urgent".

"He is one of the VVIP at this time, the security is at the highest level and no new appointments have been taken since months".

"Sophie...... It's about the survival of thousands of people and can even demolish whole of......huh", "listen, it's very very urgent, otherwise it will go out of control, it will become BIG".

"There is nothing bigger than the World War, nothing". If it's not checked, the World would not left for any wars; I have very little time......"

"I fail to understand, what are you trying to convey"?

He says while giving stress to each word "Just tell me a way to meet the scientist."

"But why should I help you? My day launched with your abuses and the rest was wasted with that nasty Officer in that dirty police station. All because of you. Tell me, why should I help you?"

He smiles "Look into my eyes, do I look like a terrorist? ......"

"Hmmm...... but promise me you will not tell anybody else."

He smiles wittily "Sure... I didn't I thought it would be that easy."

She asks while not able to listen "What?"

Burying his blunder he proceeds "Oh nothing, what were you saying".

"Ok see, the reality is completely different from what other assume. Mr. Einstein don't work at the office, His cabin is always empty and locked. It is for the security reasons".

Amar got dumbfounded and asks "So where is he?"

"He lives in his old house, there is an underground laboratory beneath his house. He stays there only, the whole day".

"I know that......"

"How you know"

"I have also seen you in his house".

"But, this fact is known only to his personal driver and some faithful officers. Officer Angus is one of them".

"Who......"

Sophie smiles "Officer Angus Clark, The one who arrested you."

"Oh No...... not him again. It's still paining, and I can't have more of him. He beat so brutally, bastard."

She asked worriedly "Really?"

"Oh not that much, leave it. We have to do something......"

"But what".

"I want to talk to him alone".

"Too risky".

"At least you can give a try......"

Sophie shook her head "Sorry, but it's not that easy".

"I have a plan......"

CH - 6

The Great abduction

Its 9 of the evening and the rain hasn't stopped yet. Nobody is seen on the roads, but the glowing lights of the Research center's office enlighten that the work is still going on.

And all of a sudden, a huddle of cars arrive the spot, making screeching noises, breaking the rhythmic silence of rain. The cars stop at the main gate of the gigantic building and Officer Clark steps out with dozen of policemen, each having an umbrella. Officer moves near the black luxury veteran car to open the door. And comes out an old man with shaggy tangled hairs and glittering personality. He could be easily recognized in the dark...... as The World famous scientist, 'Elbert Einstein'......

Officer Clark puts forth his step and commanded his policemen "Quick, follow me".

All the policemen envelop the scientist by making a ring around him and enter the workplace. They all climb the stairs making earsplitting noises with their feet.

Officer Clark opens the office door and found Sophie organizing some papers. Officer politely indicates the scientist to enter, he orders his men to stay outside the office and shuts the door.

Elbert Einstein asks courteously "Sophie, are the papers ready?"

"Yes sir, but I need 5 minutes" Sophie replied nervously.

"Take as much time as you need my child."

"No, do it fast" Officer Clark interrupts, "it's risky staying here".

Sophie feels skeptical "Okkk……"

Sophie hand over a piece of paper to the scientist. Mr. Einstein holds the paper near to his eyes and starts identifying the words.

Reading each letter Mr. Einstein speaks out loudly

To,
Franklin Roosevelt
The President of United States of America
Whi……………………………………

Officer Clark interrupts "Do it fast"

"Oh yes" Einstein replies.

With his shaking hand he took out his silver black pen and signs the letter.

"Sir I need to talk to you" Sophie says.

"Yes dear" the scientist replies.

Sophie shows some signs of hesitation through her lost expressions.

"No no, speak my child, what do you want?"

"Sir, can I take a minute of you, I want to talk to you alone, it's confidential."

"Of course, we will go…"

Officer Clark interrupts "No, it's not allowed"

"Sir, please" Sophie appeals, "it's really vital, or otherwise it would be too late…"

And the window pane smashes with entry of the Indian lad.
Amar fells on the ground with the broken pieces of glass and Officer Clark points his gun towards him and shouts "Boys…"

The policemen enters the room and get in position making Amar the target and waiting for the order to shoot.

"Stand up" Officer Clark shouts "stand up...... I knew that you would create a problem."

Amar stands while balancing himself, "Oh no" he murmurs.

Sophie turns white and thinks that she was watching Amar alive for the last time.

Showing his gun Officer Clark orders "Raise your hands Mickey Mouse, and I don't want any cleverness."

Amar raises his hands and stares at the scientist.

"Now that's what I call a good boy." Officer shouts "Now start walking."

Amar starts putting forth his step, and suddenly he leaps on Mr. Einstein and drag him to the washroom.

Tha tha tha...
Policemen start firing, but Amar locks the door. Amar throws Mr. Einstein on the toilet seat.

He asks the scientist reverently "We need to talk".

"But this is neither the right time nor the right way" scientist replies "Hmmm...... you come tomorrow morning."

Bang Bang, Tha tha tha......
All the policemen are banging the door and are firing continuously.

"Huh, yes I think you are right" says Amar.

Thak......

The door opens and the Officer enters in and found Mr. Einstein sitting on the toilet seat. Amar is not seen anywhere.

Seeing the open window Officer Clark holds scientist's hand and pulls him out "It's not safe here, we have to go."

"But... what about the letter?" asks the scientist.

"If you remain alive, we will definitely come tomorrow."

All the policemen descend down along with the scientist and her secretary, leaving the room messy.

While descending the stairs Officer Clark screams "Do fast, we need to go back".

"But sir what about the criminal" asks a Policeman.

"We will catch on him later, Mr. Einstein's life is our first priority. And I know he is not at all professional".

They all come out and Officer Clark orders "Get into the cars we will go back".

Officer opens the door of the police car and pushes the scientist inside it, but Mr. Einstein exits through the other door.

"What??"

"I will sit in my car" replies the scientist.

"Then lose your way soon". He orders a policeman "Go along with him".

"Yes Sir." The policeman replies.

Policeman holds Einstein's and Sophie's hand and darts towards the luxury car. He opens the door, tosses them on the spur of the moment and sits along them at the back seat.

"Driver, take the car to the laboratory." Policeman says.

Mr. Einstein further added "Do it fast, my life is in danger."

Driver starts the car "Sure sir, but the left wheel of the back side is puncture."

"Oh, what a stupid driver you are" policeman said "Wait, I will check".

As the policeman comes out, the officer sitting in car following, dippers the light to ask what was wrong. The policeman checks the tyres of both sides and waves his hand and shows a thumbs up conveying everything was OK. And as he turned, the car moves on. The policeman starts running behind the car.

Seeing the incidence, Officer moves his car forward, opened the door "Come in...... quick". He made him sit in and shouts "Do it Fast...... It's going to be fun......" and he puts the foot on the accelerator.

In Mr. Einstein's Car Mr. Albert Einstein gets worried "Hey stop... stop, the poor guy has left behind."

The driver moved his face back to disclose his identity. "Sorry to say sir, but you have been KIDNAPED............"

Recovering from the shock Sophie cries "W...what is this Amar?"

Amar as the disguised driver replies "Plan B......"

The policeman sitting in the officer's car starts firing.
Tha tha...

Officer Clark shouts "Hey watch out, there should be no harm to the scientist" and the officer takes out his hand out of the window and shoots.
Tha tha tha......

In the scientist's car Mr. Einstein was frightened "What's going on."

"Don't worry sir", Amar replies "I know, they are going to take full care of you". He shifts the gear of the car and turns it towards the woods.

Mr. Einstein pleads "This is wrong, God is watching, please...please leave me".

The atmosphere gets disturbed with the screeching noises of the cars.

In the police car Officer Clark says cunningly "Hahaha... I am going to enjoy the ride urrrrrr......" and he compresses the teeth.

Whoooooom......
There are three cars chasing the black luxurious one, which has the World famous Scientist.

Tha tha tha...

In the scientist's car Sophie turns to Amar and says "They are firing endlessly."

"I hope your car is bulletproof sir?" says Amar.

The city road is now over and the muddy one of the forest is chock-a-block with pits, and hence now the cars are bunking on the worn-out roads.

Feeling bumpy with bumping of the car Mr. Einstein cries "Oh God please......"

In the Police car Policeman asks the officer "Sir we are going deep inside the forest and its getting too dark".

"Shut up, will you?" shrieks the officer.

And he fires 3 more shots towards the scientist's car

Tha tha tha.......

In Mr. Einstein's Car Sophie asks "Where are we going?"

Tha tha...

Mr. Einstein asks "Oh God, save me".

The road is getting worse and the cars are joggling at the peak of their speeds.

Tha tha tha

And all of a sudden a bullet hits Amar's right shoulder "Aaaaaaaaaa...... he screams due to intense pain". And he looses his control on the steering wheel and so the car goes out of his power and goes towards a path which is completely covered with bushes.

"Oh no" Mr. Einstein screams.

Amar shouts "Oh my god".

In Police car Officer Clark says "What the hell is he doing?"

Policeman says "Sir, I think he has gone crazy, we should go back it's too late."

Officer shifts the gear and puts the foot on the accelerator to unlock the new path from where the scientist's car gets disappeared.

In Mr. Einstein's Car Mr. Einstein cries "My car..."

The car is going through the cluster of bushes, and now the branches and foliage are smashing on the front glass.

Tak tak tak......

Amar bellows "Close the windows".

"Hey, I could see something as the bushes are getting clear." Sophie says.

"What?" asks Amar.

And when the bushes swiftly get aside, they discover themselves at the edge of the cliff, and as Amar could try something, it is too late...

The car is already in a jolting speed and the car flies with the screaming noises of the innocent creature sitting inside.

Sophie "AAAAAAAA"

Amar "AAAAAAAAAAAAAA"

Mr. Einstein "AAAAAAAAAAAAAAAAAAA"

And the car lands on the elevated trees of the subordinate region and struck there.

And suddenly the officer's car also arrives the adventure spot, and the officer is able to apply the brakes disturbing the settled sand, but make a near escape and the car stops at the edge.

And suddenly following them another police car which make a smashing entry, coming on the wings and hits the officer's car. Officer opens the door and jumps to grab an exposed root at the steep of the cliff, as both the car flies with dozen of policemen inside.

On having a tight grip he observes how both the cars were smashing against the cold blooded rocks and suddenly there is a big bang.

The Officer stares at the crimson hot flames at the subordinate part. The heat can be felt near the officer, and the fire can be seen through his eyes.

At the other end, the luxurious car is landing down from on branch to the other, and when it was 2-3 feet from the ground, it struck.

"Aaah…" Amar cries "everyone is alive? I mean both of you are all right?"

"Ouch..." Sophie screams.

Mr. Einstein Tries to take out his strucked leg "Aaaa… god will punish you… aaah".

"Now don't over react, your pain is not more than mine," Amar lifts his arm "I have been shot."

"Oh no, what will you do now?" asks Sophie.

"The bullet just passed dragging the tissues along."

"Say thanks to the almighty that you are alive" Scientists says. "Otherwise the way you were driving, it felt like my last journey to hell."

"At least we are better than the two cars which were following, you should be thankful."

"Thanks for what, you mean…"

Sophie interrupts "Shut up… shut up both of you, and you Amar, I am gon...... aaah"

Mr. Einstein shows his concerned attitude "Is it paining dear?"

"Yes, a little" she replied.

"And all because of this crazy Mickey Mouse".

Amar says "Hey see..."

Sophie interrupts "You both have started over again."

Mr. Einstein "Sorry..."
Amar "Sorry..."
"Now find a way to descend down".
"Okay......" Amar replies.

At the other end the third police car reaches the end of the cliff. All the policemen come out of the car to find out for their missing colleges and their officer, and get shocked to discover him hanging on the rocks.

Policeman shouts "Bring the rescue equipments, hurry up."

They throw the ladder down towards the steep.

Policeman shouts "Sir... sir, hold the ladder, sir."
The officer gingerly comes up climbing the ladder and then collapse on the ground. He is breathing heavily.

Officer Clark utters in wobbly voice "Www... water... water."

The policeman gives him a water bottle from his bag.

His drinking oodles of water is justified by the fact that he is hanging for quite a time on the deadly cliff and the blistering smoke of burning cars packed with ashes are knocking his face for pretty long.

Officer manages to stands up, washes his face and roars "Contact the headquarters......"

CH - 7

The convincement

All three are now out of the luxury car, gawking at its broken headlights, broken bonnet, broken glasses etc. etc. etc……

"Pity on me, my dear car" The scientist sees the car's condition.

And he starts screening his agony through his tears. Sophie points Amar to aid the scientist.

Amar pace close to the scientist "Hey see… sorry … I had no option. I didn't know where the hell your car was going."

"You just remain quite", said the scientist. "You know what you have done??? Why me??? I have no money to give. Please...please leave me."

"Sir no...no no, you are getting me wrong. Just... please..."

"No......" he interrupts, "You should first know, what the hell you have done... I am not an eminent personality but... I am appointed as the Research Head in this country, and I am damn important for the government. That's why they have provided me such a tight security. You would be trapped in all this, you are of my son's age, and it's really very complicated. I advice you... leave me now... and I guarantee, there would be no arrest. Otherwise you would be in a big dilemma, which I don't want...... You know, what big callous crime you have commited, you would be liable for the bombarding of the police jeeps, and the death of those policeman".

Amar takes a deep breath, closes his eyes and watches up in the sky "Sorry sir, I couldn't keep your promise..."

"Whom are you talking to? Please leave me, I had gone to office for signing the letter, which was extremely important, I can't leave that as it is, the letter needs to be sent without any delay."

"And what is in the letter?"

"Nothing of your business. It's a highly confidential pivotal job."

"And your pivotal job is going to make a big bang, (laying stress on each word) the bang that you will regret the whole life".

Mr. Einstein gets thunderstruck "What??????"

"Yes sir, the research, for which you are sweating day and night, working with so much integrity, the research you think going to be used in a constructive direction, is going to take lives of lakhs of innocent people".

Scientist's level of astonishment increased "What are you saying???"

"Yes, the kind of energy that you are going to produce through your chemical reactions, will be used as an atom bomb to bombard Hiroshima and Nagasaki in Japan".

"Oh no", his expressions reveals his bewilderment. "I can't... b..but they promised me... we had a contract".

Amar laughs "Hahaha... you know? You are such a good person, But the bloody world is too evil for the existence of goodness...... Your talent is being misused Mr. Einstein......"

"No, no, no, it's wrong, I don't believe it...... It can't be possible, you are lying".

"I can't lie".

"I don't believe you young boy. You think you going to utter any rubbish, and I would node my head readily like a small child. (Showing inquisitiveness) I think it's your plan, are you from the soviet group?"

"Apply brakes on your mouth scientist. I have a proof......"

"What?" asks Sophie, "proof?"

"oh really" scientist's approach projects as if he is taking it lightly, "a proof sounds interesting".

"Ok then, here you go" he puts his hands inside his inner coat and took out a paper and forwards it to Mr. Einstein, "Have a look".

"What's this?" Mr. Einstein crouches his eyes.

"Hah... proof" Amar answers assertively.

"What?"

"Read it out, it's a newspaper".

"Sorry I can't......"

"Now what happened, scientist?" he asks "Got scared?"

"Hey I am not one of them. The thing is that I don't have my specs..."

"Sir, the specs is in your right pocket" said Sophie.

The scientist starts locating his spectacles in his coat, "where is it" and shows some sign of relief as he found them "Thanks dear..."

She smiles "It's my duty sir."

He smiles back "So nice of you..."

Amar starts making awkward faces "All the formalities are over? Can you read the newspaper now, Your Highness..."

Changing his beam into revulsion looks, he wears his specs and flats the newspaper.

Sophie interrupts due to over splitting inquisitiveness "Please read it loudly".

Amar folds his hands under his arms and the scientist starts reading the newspaper.

"The whole world trembled again when the atom bomb was bombarded on Nagasaki. It recreates the devastation occurred in Hiroshima on 5 February 1945. It's suspected that lakhs of peo......"

Sophie interrupts "What... what's the date... what's the date you just read?"

Mr. Einstein crouches his eyes and runs his fingers on the paper "...in Hiroshima on February 1945......" he ponders while making a weird face "What is this? I am asking what is this?...... You are showing me the newspaper of the year yet to come and... are we fools, do you..."

Amar interrupts "Hey just listen..."

Mr. Einstein cuts again "What type of prank is this, you are caught young man."

"Huh...... ok, we need to have a talk".
"What else we are doing."

"No... its getting very frosty we need to find a shelter it's too dark now".
"You can't leave it like this..." says Sophie.
"And we can't even leave my car ..." Mr. Einstein adds.

"Ok, we will stay here only," Amar dusts away his pants "I will manage the fire". He lifts his eyes to observe the jungle as far as he can, and as stands up Sophie interrupts him,
"Where, where are you going? What about the newspaper?" she screams when he doesn't reacts "What I am asking?"

"I am not leaving" he answers, "just going to fetch some wood. And the entire night is there for disclosing the mystery, have patience dear...... Just wait and watch."

CH - 8

Disclosure of the anonymity

The world had yet to listen a 'BREAKING NEWS', and which spreads like a fire. Every Radio, every News Chanel has one pivotal news to reveal, 'Famous Scientist Elbert Einstein Kidnapped.'

The news till now has knocked the doors of every country -Russia, U.S.A, China, India, Africa, Japan......, making lots of open mouth expressions all over the globe. The world is shaken......

And why not the news should make headlines? The so called 'The Kidnapper' has killed dozens of policemen, with kidnapping the world famous scientist,

his secretary, it was also believed that scientist's lost
driver is also killed, and attempt to murder, in the case
of the officer, as it was told by Officer Angus Clark.
And according to the officer, he has all the
rights to make 'big' 'BIGGER', because
he has lost his policemen, his dignity, and
somewhere mercy for the Indian man.
He is after him like anything. All the faithful
policemen are assigned for the job.
The kidnaper is believed to be arrested very soon......

Till now, quite a well preparation is done for spending a night, lots of dry grass, with a bone fire in the centre. It resembles to the curiosity shown by kids while they make preparations and get ready to sit around their grandmother for listening fairy tales......

And both the scientist and her secretary sit near Amar, around the fire,

"hmmm...... So..." Amar proceeds "I am here to stop you, from sending your letter to president of U.S.A., Franklin Roosevelt for your approval to use your research".

"I..."

"Should I first complete... sir......" Amar interrupts the scientist in between, "please......"

"But..."

"Please......" he interrupts again.

"Hmmm......" scientist crossed his arms.

"Your approval will cause devastation, or may be THE END of the world in the future...... I know you don't rely on me, so I have shown you the newspaper, you didn't even rely on that. So... so I have to tell you something of 'ME', my story, ... my experience which brings me here".

Sophie "hmmm..."

"Sure...... continue, I want to listen......" scientist says".

"I am from France" Amar proceeds, "my parents, whom I have never seen, were from India, I was brought up in an orphanage in France...... I am a historian, in fact an assistant historian.

"Oh, so you have a job." The scientist smiles "I thought you would be a terrorist or something like that".

"Hehe..." Amar laughs phonically, "It was not at all funny..."

"Oh ho", Sophie interrupts. "You please proceed..."

"Hmm... I am an assistant Historian, and I was given a task to investigate at the 'Old fort of France'."

"The same fort which is famous for the lost door mystery?" Sophie asks.

"Yes..." Amar smiles.

"How do you know about it?" Mr. Einstein asks Sophie.

"I had read about it somewhere, it is said that years ago, one of the two main doors got missing, and since then the fort has only one door".

"Exactly," Amar proceeds, "and I had to investigate that fort, and one day, when I was investigating......

"Phrush phrush...... the dust from the walls of THE OLD FORT OF FRANCE flied away as I was employing the brush, standing on a ladder with brush in one hand a notebook in the other.

Aaaanchhee ....

"Huh... oh so it was you, I got scared with your sneeze, dear"

I said to my friend who had just arrived, we both share the same age.

"Oh what is this Amar, I had ringed you so many a times but you didn't picked up"

Sophie interrupts in between "What?"

"Yes..." Amar smiles.
"You mean... she looks same as me?"
"Yes"
"Oh My GOD!"

"Now, I hope it justify my behavior at your office, that's why I got amazed."

"Oh my God, it's just like a miracle, I would like to meet her" Sophie replies overwhelmingly.

"No no no... not now".

"Please..."

Amar continues the story "I put my hand inside my coat's pocket and took my cell out and said...

"Oh yes, I am very sorry Meghana. It was on silent."

"Whatever, I think we should have a coffee together, are you free?" Meghana asks.

"Does it look like...... The day I fall in love with you, MADAM... that day my life was ruined. And now I think, I have to lose my job too. And for your kind information, I don't like coffee at all".

"Mr. Historian, I quit and you win. Now come on, we will have something else. And you also have an appointment with the doctor". She took out a piece of paper from her bag and shows it to me, it was an appointment slip of Dr. Soni at 3:00 on 25 March 2014. "Have you forgotten my 'MICKEY MOUSE'???"

"Oh yes, I had nearly forgotten, THANKS.... But dare u call me 'MICKEY MOUSE'"

"Hahaha", Meghana laughed, "sorry ......"

Mr. Einstein Interrupts in between "Wh wh what?????? 2012? Are we fool. NO, no, I don't want to listen to this rubbish, no, I am going" and he stands up.

"Sir please" Amar holds his hands.

"No, leave me, I don't want to listen all this, I am not a kid that you can make a fool out of me", the scientist starts getting heated up "I said, leave me".

"So be a kid for sometime, please for God sake".

"No, leave me or I will kill you."

"Sir please......" Sophie interrupts.

"He is just speaking anything" Mr. Einstein screams.

"Please sir, I feel he is honest and trying to say something, maybe something good for you".

"Ok, I got it. He is from the future centaury. Then how did he come here? Do you mean to say, he had used a Time Machine? Are you......" And he stops and gets gopsmacked "No it can't be possible. He has the newspaper, oh my God..."

"You have been caught Mr. Scientist" Amar says.

"Oh no..." scientist holds his head.

"Hahaha, now keep quit and listen" Amar laughs.

"What happened?" asks Sophie.

"Haha... nothing" Amar gazes towards the scientist)

Amar continues the story
"Oh yes, I had nearly forgotten, THANKS.... But dare u call me 'MICKEY MOUSE'"

"Hahaha, sorry ......" Meghana

I put my equipments in the kit and walked away with my girlfriend.

CH - 9

And the tale starts

The fire is getting milder and so Amar is breaking small branches kept beside him and is throwing into the bon fire, the scientist is rubbing his hands to make himself more comfortable in the uncomfortable chilly surrounding and Sophie is gazing Amar continuously with a smile on her face.

After getting aware of the fact that he is being starred Amar asks Sophie "Hey!" he waves his hands to disturb her eye contact "where are you roaming, lady?"

"Oh! Sorry" She feels shy and handled her hairs behind ears.

"Ahem ahem" realizing that it could get worse "so... so we left the palace, and she took me to a psychiatrist".

"Psychiatrist" the scientist puts stress on the word "Psychiatrist hahaha…so I was right, that you are nuts, hahaha…"

"It was not at all funny, scientist" making weird faces.

"Haha…sorry, you carry on…"

Amar continues the story "Meghana drove me to Dr. Soni's clinic, an Indian psychiatrist".

"So Mr. Rathore, you are late." Dr. Soni said.

"Wh wh what doctor… you mean… How much time I am left with??????"

"Oh no, you are not getting it, I mean your appointment was at 3 o'clock and you have arrived at 4." Dr. Soni said "By the way, your reports are normal, and I think you are fit… then what type of problem you are facing?"

"Nothing serious doctor, but I am fed up with a particular Dream that I see, almost every day."

"Can you tell me more".

"Doctor, it is like, I am lost in a cave, or moreover a palace, yes right, 'a palace', and I see… statues, lots and lots of statues, and they look like, they want to talk to me, it's like, I don't know but they are…huh……"

"Take a breath" Dr. Soni gave me a glass of water "have it". As I finished of the glass he proceed "What are you wearing in your right hand Mr. Rathore".

"It's a bracelet doctor".

"But it looks like an old antique gadget, from where you get it?"

"It was stumbled on by my dog, when I was exploring a primordial fort".

"See Mr. Rathore, you are a Historian by profession, a person who indulges in the past, so I think, your Life is being mixed in your profession. I would request you to take rest and give time to family and your dear ones. And see how that everything goes on its respective track" he smiled "And take this chit to the receptionist, she will give you the medicine".

"Thank you doctor".

"I hope you get well soon..." and Dr. Soni smiled.

CH-10

Not so good morning

Amar rubs his hands "That night Meghana stayed at my home".

"Which night?" asks Mr. Einstein.

"What??????" Sophie asks in a shock.

Amar answers the scientist "That very night".

"What do you mean? She slept with you?" Sophie asks again.

"Aaa… Yes", says Amar why are you so over reacting?'

Sophie gives an irritated look "Nothing".

"Hey, that's the Twenty first century, it's not a big deal".

"Fine" Sophie replies irritably, "continue..."

"Ok... so we spend the night together, and she left in the morning, early, I was still sleeping, the clock strike 9 and the alarm was ringing since half an hour. The alarm was getting louder and louder, but I was in a yawning nap".

And to add to my tragedy, my dog woke up. He ran and jumped upon my bed. He barked, and then barked heavily............ No response.

He started jumping on the bed to wake me up, but when nothing happened...... he pissed on my face......

......

"Hun...... ooolurphh......phhhuu.............. eleaaa yak ....oh shit" I woke up. "What the hell have you done Scott? I mean... Can't you find a healthier way? It's so ... eleaaa. Oh my GOD! I need to go to the washroom".

"You need to see the clock dad. You are late." Scott barked.

Sophie interrupts the narration "What did you said?"

"Now please, don't tease me" Amar replies.

"No, you said that your dog speaks".

"I didn't say anything like that".

Scientist says "Yes, you did but..."

Amar gives a weird look "I don't like interruptions guys, please."

"Ok sorry" Sophie holds her ears.

"But what you said?" asks the scientist "What his name was? Scott?"

"Yes, now can I continue?"

Amar continues the story

"Hey just stop barking and …huh, Already I am fed up with these nightmares in my dream, and you know you are such a…"

"See the clock dad." Scott pointed towards the wall clock.

I looked at the clock "Oh my GOD, it's 9:30, I am late."

I just went inside the washroom, washed my face and left with my old dirty clothes. I ran outside towards my scooter. I kicked, kicked hard, but no response from the second hand product. I left the scooter with its key and ran to find any taxi. Taking the advantage of a scooter with the key, a person just joined its wires which he had broken five minutes before. He sat on it, made a witty face to Scott, who was watching all this, and ran away. To save his master's scooter, Scott also loped after the thief. If anyone can't leave even a second hand scooter how could anyone leave an open house? So in few minutes, thieves' cohorts entered the house, one by one they evacuated the goods, and scuttled away.

On the other hand not finding any taxi due to the transport strike, and even not finding a good human being, who was ready to give a lift, I decided to go by foot. I was running hastily as I was missing a train, and perhaps I missed it too.

CH-11

Good bye Mickey Mouse!

"Breathing heavily and full of sweat, I was able to reach the railway station, I mean 'The Society of French Historical'. I entered and rushed to the core office. Before I could open the door, door opened and came out my most ghastly colluege, with broad glasses and a broader smile on his face.

"Hey Munish, what happen inside?" I asked him.

"Just go and check it on your own my MICKEY MOUSE." Was the reply that I got.

Interrupting the narration, Amar says "He was the one whom I misinterpreted with your Officer Clark..."

"Hehehehe" Sophie giggles as she couldn't stop her laugh.

"Oh my God... Haha" the scientist chuckles too.

Amar smiles "Hey now stop giggling, then I asked him what happened inside?"

"Just go and check it on your own Mr. MICKEY MOUSE". Munish, my colluege replied.

"Dare you call me that" I said firmly.

"Puuchhh... somebody is waiting for you inside. Now get lost".

I went inside and found, Mr. Mehta, a long handsome gentleman and my BOSS.

"Good morning Sir".

He was busy reading the newspaper. The newspapers were filled that day with news of shettring of share market and the chaos created by the transporters at the Boulevard Haussmann road.

"Rathore... have a seat" Mr. Mehta indicated towards the chair and removed his glasses.

"It's ok sir".

"So... I am very sorry to say, but you are late".

"I am very sorry, sir, it was a transport strike today, but I think am just half an hour late".

"I am not talking about that, gentleman." He stood and took the cup of coffee in his hands. "I want to say that the time given to you for the investigation of the 'OLD FORT' is now over, but no report is given to me till now. So ... Munish Byala is going with us to the Egypt project. Better luck next time."

"But..."

"And one more thing, if you feel like then you can remain as a part of our association, but we would be unable to give you salary from today, and... you have to vacant company's apartment too. Best of LUCK".

"Sir, but, but it's my dream to work with you, it's my dream to go to 'Egypt'... I beg of you..."

"Hey, hey... I can't help you, it's not my decision, so... ok bye, I hope we will meet soon".

"Sure sir..." I came out with a low head and...

"So what happen inside Mickey Mouse?" Munish was standing in front of me revolving his car key in his index finger.

"**** you, get LOSS....."

Munish pushed me and I fell on the table behind, I stood up but Munish picked me from my collar and gave me a blow on my nose. My nose started bleeding, and before I could recover that, Munish threw me on the floor and punt me twice on my stomach. The spectators sensed that it could result to worse, so two of them hold Munish from his back, but the wild monster was impending towards me as if he was going to filch my life away. My colleague directed me to go back.

CH-12

A strange visitor

Watching the overcast sky Amar proceeds "That day, the weather was just like today...... exactly the same... The strike was still on, and I had no means to get back home, I was wounded, every fraction of mine was in pain, which was quite visible from my walk. The weather was getting worse and worse, and I could see an arrival of a storm......"

It was getting dark, and that day I was late, I saw Scott sitting on the doorsteps with his slack face on his paws.

"Hey, what happened, why my boy is so sad?" I asked him.

Scott didn't move and didn't speak anything.

I sat on my knees beside him "Hey wh...... 'Oh My God', shit, I forget to give you your food, oh I am so sorry, but even I haven't eaten anything, let's go inside, we will have the dinner together".

"I wish if only the hunger was the problem......" Scott barked. "Come in dad, I will tell you. And he stood up, pulled my pants and told me to follow him.

"What happened? What you want??? Hey...what happened?......" And as I entered the house, I saw that all my belongings became imperceptibly extinct from the picture "'Oh my God', what the hell... oh crap, where all the things went??????"

He barked in a cheerless tone "They are not here dad, they stole them, I am sorry..."

Realizing that I left with the door unlocked in the morning "Oh no, its... it's all my fault, I left the house unlocked, and..." giving a short thought "hey wait, my scooter" and I rushed towards the window. "Where is my scooter" and I ran outside towards the door, the scooter was nowhere "Oh I have lost it, I have lost it too".

Scott brought a piece of cloth "Papa I bite hard on his leg, that bastard, but he ran".

"And you... you were watching all this like a climax of a movie. But... but I know, it's entirely my fault, I have shouldn't called Meghana last night... I couldn't wake up early and all this happened. She is just..."

Tring Tring, Tring Tring

The phone call interrupts

I went to pick up the call "Hello"

"Hi!" Meghana was at the other side. "What are you doing dearo… I am missing you too much my Mickey Mouse, where are you?"

"Sitting inside the pressure cooker" I replied in rage, "want to join me… get lost and don't ever call me. Bye".

"But where are you going?" she innocently asked.

I screamed "In the hell……"

Thuphhh… I threw away the cell phone on the floor.

"Dad has gone mad" Scott barked.

"Come here Scott" I stretched my hands towards him.

Scott came to me and sat on my lap.

I placed my chin on his head, "I am left with nothing, nothing, my job, my house, lost everything. Not even a penny, crap…." And I banged my hand hard on the ground, and it sounded unusual, like something was under that wooden floor.

"Dad, I think something is under it".

"Scott, I think something is under it…… go and bring a screw driver".

Scott ran and holds the kit with his mouth and comes back to me.

"Now you get aside, you may get hurt".

Aaunch aaunch...

I started loosening the screws of the planks, slowly and slowly... I removed the planks one by one.

"Come on dad..." I barked while jumping.

I removed the planks and then swept away the sand. And... to my astonishment... it was a huge wooden plank... with something engraved on it.

"Oh no, it's a wooden board, I thought we would hit upon with a buried bone, shit man."

"I couldn't control the queer thrill "Oh my God, it's not an ordinary piece of wood Scott, it looks like... like an ancient door...of some ancient place...... Scott... bring my kit".

"Is there any secret basement beneath it? And I think it would be filled with flesh ... bones... cookies..."

"Stop blaring and go, till then I will take it out".

I removed the other planks and then took the door out, it was heavy like anything. I somehow managed to make it stand towards the wall.

Holding the kit in his mouth Scott arrived "here I am", and he tossed the kit on the floor.

I took out my equipments and started clearing the glued dust and algae which was developed on that door. I cleaned it with some liquids and then used a cloth to make it dry. Then I took out a magnificent glass to check what anomalous thing it was, and suddenly I turned and took my bag in my hands and started finding something in my files.

And all of a sudden the file slipped from my hands.

"Oh my God... Oh my God...... I can't believe this, The Old Fort of France... The mystery is solved... Yesss"

Scott barked "what?"

Interrupting the narration, Sophie asks "What?"

Khaaan fhuuu... khaaan fhuuu......

The scientist is sleeping with his mouth wide open.

"Oh no, I haven't seen such an irritating personality..." says Amar "I think you are not interested in listening to my story, I think I am turning your mood off".

"No no, not at all," says Sophie. "In fact it's too interesting, every word you utter, make my inquisitiveness more wild and sturdy. Tell me, please?"

Amar blushes "What?"

"What about the lost door? So you find it under your house..."

"I can't reveal it now, let the scientist come out of his dreams."

"Please..." Sophie appeals.

"Till then..."

Sophie blushes "Till then what?"

"Till then, I should go and fetch something to eat".

"No you are not going anywhere."
Amar turned his eye brows up.
"I... I am just scared, that's it" she cleared.

"I have to go, we can't remain without food and water the whole night." He tries to stand by using his injured arm as a support and suddenly he cries out. "Ouch!"

Sophie immediately rushes towards him "What happened?"

Amar holds his arm tightly "I was hit by a bullet while the policemen were chasing us in the car".

"Oh Jesus, why the hell you were quiet about this, and even I forget to ask it from you, is it still hurting?"

"Hey, nothing to worry, the bullet just passed, perturbing some of the upper skin folds, no big reason to worry about, please calm down".

"It's still bleeding, are you making fool of me, remove your coat..."

"What???" he asks.

Sophie gives him a livid look "Remove it... Now ..."

"Ok ok... I am doing it". He starts removing his cloth but its sleeve got struck to an ambiguous thingamajig type watch he was wearing in his right hand.

"Wait, I will help you!"

"No no, stay away, I.. I will see to it".

"But what queer thing is this?" she asks.

While removing his coat he says "Its nothing, you don't need to be fret, I am completely fine... aaaaa......" And he screams due to instant pain in his arm.

On seeing his shirt colored in blood Sophie asks in expletively "This is what u call fine? Are you mad, remove it now".

"What".

"Your shirt..."

"Are you mad, how can..."

She comes close to him and start unbuttoning his shirt "Being your friend I have the right to do this". Amar goes gopsmacked and is not in a condition to reply.

She supports his arm with her hands "Lift your arms, slowly......the wound is really very deep, do you have a hanky?"

"Wh..."

She interrupts "Wait I have one", and she takes out the scarf she was wearing around her neck, and she ties it tightly on his arm.

"Ouch!..."
Sophie holds his arm with care and kissed it.
Amar stands up immediately "I am going".

"You are not going anywhere", and she holds his hand. "You are going to sit with me".

"Let me go..."

Sophie also stands up "I will not let you go alone...... ...... I will accompany you?"

"What about the scientist?"

She blushes "leave him, he is perfectly fine. Let's go".

Amar smiles and holds her hand "the jungle gets cruel at this time, so... stay here".

Sophie lowers her eyes and says "When I am with you, I don't know why, but I feel like I am safe......"

He put a step towards her and gingerly came close to her "I can't put your life in danger, I can't afford it..."

Suddenly she hugs him tightly……

And a drop of tear runs down Amar's cheek, he holds her face, Sophie lift her hands and wipes his cheeks, he holds her hands and gazes into her eyes, comes close to her and she closes her eyes. And out of the blue Amar notices some movement behind the bushes, and suddenly a man jumps out firing a bullet from his riffle, Amar pushes Sophie as the bullet passes between them.

Amar rushes towards her to pick her up when suddenly…

"Stop or I will shoot"

Standing before them was a tall lean man in brown uniform with rifle in his hands.

Amar goes dumbfounded and asks "Doctor?"

The thin man replies "Doctor doesn't keep guns, kid."

"Now don't say he looks like your psychiatrist…" says Sophie.

Amar nods his head.

"Minutes ago I had heard about the scientist's kidnapping on the radio" says the thin man, "and now, hahaha… I have caught the kidnapper".

Sophie comes forward "Please leave us officer, he…."

Thin man interrupts and smiles amusingly "It sounds good, but I am here to hunt, I am a hunter... so... Hands up".

Amar get frightened "h h…hunter???... you kill a..animals???... you know its banned".

"Bans are for children, not for me... and don't act too smart, turn around, on your knees" says the hunter.

Sophie shouts "Tiger!" And she points towards the hunter's back.

Petrified Amar asks "What... where?"

The Hunter turns back and swiftly Sophie grabs a dagger which is hanging outside Amar's Pants and holds a tight grip of hunter's neck from his back.

"Here you go, drop your gun" yells Sophie.

Amar gets shocked "Vo vo vo... Lady, easy easy..."

Sophie kicks on hunter's knees "drop your gun and hands up".

The hunter does the same" See... it's not right... I.. I mean" and Sophie tightens her grip at his neck.

"Hey.. hey.. wait.. it hurts... mummy..." and the hunter starts crying. "Please leave me, I didn't wanted to come in the woods at night, leave me, I.. I beg you......"

Amar gets surprised "What?"

Hunter cries "Today, when I and my wife were shopping in the market, a thieve snatched my wife's purse, she ordered me to ran behind him, I did the same, but.." he wipes his tears with the sleeve of his shirt. "But when I got a hold of him, he snatched my watch and my wallet too, so..." sobs. "She throw me out of the house to roam around in this daunting forest in so dark, I was just roaming and finding a shelter, please..."

Sophie interrupts "I can't believe you call yourself a hunter".

"Please leave me, I beg of you please".

"Leave her Sophie", Amar appeals. "I think he is telling the truth". And Sophie pushes him.

Hunter starts breathing heavily "Haaaa haa!... Thank you haa haaa...... Please madam, sir... do me a favor, I can't go home back as it is too dark, and you are well aware about the wild ani..."

Amar interruptsing and places his hands on hunter's shoulders "Don't worry bro, be calm, you can stay with us"
While seeing stunningly towards Sophie he says "I never thought that you would be ... I mean you are so daring".

Sophie smiles "Thank You." She gives Amar his dagger "It seems to be a royal one, where you get it?"

"It's a long story......"

"Hey" hunter barges in while unpacking his bag. "Do you want to eat something, I have some sandwiches..."

"My my my, that's what my ears were dying to listen", says Amar. "Take it out."

"Tell me about your knife" Sophie asks for the second time.

"Some other day dear", he replied. "Now go and wake the scientist up, he may be also hungry. What's your name daring hunter"?

"Raman…" he replied.

"Aawwhhh… a..and what after the lost dooor the scientist wakes up and stretches his arms. Rubbed his eyes and yawns again … "Aawwhhh…"

"Yes, yes Mr. Scientist we will continue", says Amar. "But sit and have something to eat".

Mr. Einstein gets dazed "What, where, how?"

"Now leave that", says Amar. "Come on!"

The scientist stands up gingerly sporting his frail back and goes towards Sophie and gets surprised to see a new member
"Who is this ring master?"

"Good morning sir" Raman says. "I mean Good evening sir, I am so glad I mean I am seeing you alive for the first time".

The scientist gives strange looks "Who is this?"

Amar hilariously smiles "He is sponsoring tonight's dinner 'Your Highness'."

"Who are you?" asks Mr. Einstein. "May be your gang member, Amar?"

"Why is he staring like this?" asks Raman.

"Nothing pivotal sir" replies Sophie, "he was roaming just here and we thought he will prove to be a good company".

Mr. Einstein stares towards Raman) I don't think so".

Raman passes a piece of bread to the scientist "Bread".

"Fine, Thanks, Now can we ensue, what after the door." Says the scientist.

Amar proceeds "So..."

"Which door?" Raman asks.

Amar gets fumed up "ahhh... I don't like these interruptions, you are watching the movie after the intermission so please remain quit".

Raman "Finger on the lips".

CH-13

That Palace in the obscurity

Being an outsider, and even after attacking them, the hunter is able to create a place between the queer gathering. It is astounding that why a person who came to catch the kidnapper was now a part of them and at the same time it is as surprising to see that how they became ready to give him a shelter. Ignoring this fact, each one of them is sitting around the bon fire discussing history, investigating it and may be getting prepare to create it.

"I took out the door that was beneath my house," Amar heralds. "I cleaned it and inquire my files to find from where it belongs and all of a suddenly...

The file slipped from my hands "Oh my God... Oh my God...... I can't believe this, The Old Fort of France... The mystery is solved... Yesss..."

Amar interrupt the narration "'The Old Fort of France'... The mystery which I solved was the lost main door. The main door of the fort had two doors, out of which 1 was stolen long ago, may be two hundred-three hundred years, and I found it under my house".

Scott barked "What?"

I picked the door vigilantly and kept it again inside the floor and fix the planks on it so that it remains safe until I return.

I took the bag on my back

"We need to go now Scott, come on. Wait... should we lock the doors?" Scott started making weird faces "Leave it, there is nothing left to be stoled".

And the weather got worse than the trepidation, it started raining......

I took an umbrella and we both stepped out and put our feet towards the Old Fort. The fort was 15 minutes away from my house, and I took a shortcut from cremation ground. The storm was so lethal that my umbrella flew away. It was so frosty and at the same time so bloodcurdling that we both were wavering like anything. I took Scott in my lap and was running on the double towards the fort.

As we were coming close to that ancient palace, optically I could see it getting bigger, similarly was escalating the feeling that it's going to be something really dangerous and intimidating. And we both were standing right in the front of the palace which I never thought looked so scary at night. The lightening in the sky made it easy for the palace to be visible in the dark and difficult for us to enter it.

Terrified Scott barks "I am not going to enter inside." He was trying to jump off from my lap.

"What are you doing, let's go" I commanded.

We both put forth our steps expecting that we had not committed a mistake by coming there. And the first thing that came our way was the main gate at the entrance, with ample space for the missing one, which was under my house, and which brought me here. I took out my torch to investigate it properly.

Scott was incessantly pulling my trousers. He was panicking as much as he could "Dad, let's go, what are we doing here".

"Shhhhhh.... Quit, believe me" I said with my wide open eyes. "We are going to make history".

I went further, there was a big dining table with chairs right in the center of the hall, but to my astonishment, it was not looking the same palace which I used to visit every day during the light. There was a big lamp on the table, with lots of candlesticks kept alongside. It was really astonishing why things were kept in such a manner.

And suddenly a sound came from upstairs, breaking my concentration, I climb up the stairs and rotate my neck left right to see what happened. A portrait was fallen, may be due to the storm outside, I picked it up and clean it with my hands. It was the portrait of Queen Elizabeth.

I hung the portrait from where it belong, but Queen Elizabeth was not the only one who embellish the palace, there were lot many portraits hung on the wall, with the numerous Eminent personalities breathing in them. Alexander The Great, Mahatma Gandhi, Shaheed Bhagat Singh, Mughal Emperor Jalal-u-din Mohammad Akbar, King Ashoka and Scientist Elbert Einstein and many more......

While I was observing the Portraits I saw reflection of some light on the glass of one of them, I turned, and it was a bronze cross worn by a colossal statue of Jesus Christ, I went near it with inquisitive eyes. The dull brown statue was of the same height as mine, with open hands as if God is showering his blessings.

I just scratched the cross to remove the unwanted dust, and as I lift my eyes, I saw that the eyes of Jesus start shining and the color changed to green.

I got astounded and opened my hands in astonishment, and to add to my astonishment, the statue smiled, descends his hands and clapped on my hands.

My color changed to white and my breath stopped when it started laughing, louder and louder......

Thrash thaa etc etc...

All the glasses of the windows smashed and it started sparking inside the palace and the storm become worse and looks like as it had entered the palace itself.

I ran to save my life, but as I was descending from the stairs, my foot slipped and I fell down, rolling on the stairs. I managed to stand up and started running towards outside. I came out and fell on the ground......

Today it had crossed all the limits of dreadfulness, but it was not the end, I realized that I had left Scott inside......

"Oh shit, shit, where is Scott, oh no......" I shouted so that he could came out, listening my voice. "Scott... Scott... Oh no... I have to go in... Oh...... relax, relax... Inhale, exhale... Yes, you can do it......"

After gathering some courage and consciousness, I went inside. "S..S. Scott... Scott."

And to my astonishment I saw spots of blood on the floor which were heading towards the dining table where I saw Scott lying on swathe with blood......

"'Oh my God'......" I cried.

And as I said these words, there was a drastic change in the surrounding. The chandelier started glittering and the candles on the candlesticks that were kept on the table got lit. The dirt from the walls, portraits and everything got detached, fell on the ground, and goes out of the door with the leaves......

But...... the most noticeable and astounding change that appeared, was......

'All the people who were having there portraits hanging in the palace...... Were sitting on the dining table'......

CH-14

The souls

As I said those words, there was a drastic change in the surrounding, all the people who were having there portraits hanging in the palace were sitting on the dining table.

"Wha... Oh no..." I got stunned.

I tried to turn around to run out of that inhuman place, but I slipped and fall on the wet floor, but as I stood up again and strived to run, an intense voice stopped my way.

A man wearing clothes and jewelry which belong to Mughal era raised his left hand and said...

"One more step you take and I am going to kill your dog".

And I stood still with closed eyes

Then a person wearing a dirty grey coat, with black tie and untidy hears and more scary mustache, something something like you Mr. Einstein.

The scientist interrupts his narration and says "Now, now I caught you red handed".

Amar gets irritated "Now what"?

"You mean that I would be alive in the twenty first century, haha I caught you".

"Please for heaven sake keep quit and listen".

"What I didn't get it". asks Raman.

"Then just listen instead of disturbing your grey cells", to himself. "Oh my God I just hate these interruptions. So... Mr. Einstein stood up and said......"

Mr. Einstein said "Hey... boy, relax, he is alive, come sit here, don't worry he is just sleeping, come on young man..."

And then an Indian young man with alluring mustache, wearing a cowboy hat came near me. He hold my hand and took me near the dining table. He was just like the Bhagat Singh which I saw in the portrait.

He said "Hey brother, you can sit with ease, lighten up your mind".

I slowly sat on the chair, everyone was continuously starring at me... and all of a sudden I stood up. "I.. I am sorry, but I need to go".

Emperor Akbar said "Your dog..."

But I interrupted "No... no problem, you can keep him, he is an obedient dog, he will not disturb you. Ok bye".

And a person wearing ancient roman clothes and a diadem, and dressed like Alexander the Great, hold my hand, "Young man, that's it? You have such a weak heart, you don't like surprises or adventures. Sit, we need to talk".

As I sat, a beautiful old lady in a royal dress lifted her head high and spoke

"To start today's discussion, and to solve the dilemmas of this poor child, I, Queen Elizabeth want...

I interrupted again "Hey hey wait, you want to say that you are Queen Elizabeth, and I am..."

Emperor Akbar interrupted me "Shhhhhh..."

"I just..."

"Do not interrupt... Yes, Your Highness..." said Emperor Akbar.

"I, Queen Elizabeth, want my council to guide this boy about our caucus. And now, I want Mr. Gandhi to proceed".

Mahatma Gandhi: Thank you madam. Listen my child, as you know, we are popular figures in the history, who are not alive...

Mr. Einstein interrupts the narration in between "Oh... I didn't noticed that some of the personalities are dead since centuries. So you mean I was also...... we all are spirits?"

Amar gets fully irritated "Ugh ... it's the limit scientist. Your disruptions are worse than the speed breakers".

"But..."

Amar interrupts "Yes you were a spirit".

"Why would my spirit revolves in an old fort?"

The scientist is getting on his nerves "Please scientist".

Sophie says "It's going to be something big".

Amar continues the story "And then he introduced me to others".

Mahatma Gandhi said "She is the most Powerful women in the History – Queen Elizabeth, sitting beside you is the triumphant Mughal Emperor Jilal-ul-din Mohammad Akbar", she pointed through his hands "he is Shaheed Bhagat Singh, Great scientist Elbert Einstein, Alexander The Great and the all time man of power, Ashoka.

King Ashoka added “Thank you sir. We all are here due to the desire of the almighty. The people who make history through their endeavors or change it, and make people love them, becomes a part of our convention. It’s the weight of the aspirations of people’s faith on our souls, it’s their love, their anticipations, their belief that force us to remain here among them even after our bereavement”.

Alexander the Great said “We all sit together, discuss together the comings and goings of the world that arise of late”.

“And then we all came to one conclusion and take action, if the obstacle is under our reach” said Emperor Akbar.

Queen Elizabeth declares “Our council is a group of few. It’s very much possible that many dead aficionadas of this soil may be sitting in an old daunting fort like we are, and may be discussing the predicaments of the human race…”

“Ok…” I said.

Emperor Akbar asks “What ok? You don’t believe us?”

“I didn’t say so” I said.

“Ok then...” He took out a dagger out of his pocket, I got startled and he said “Don’t’ agonize, its not to kill you”.

And he threw the knife up in the air and it descends down and hit an apple lying front of me, cutting it into 4 even pieces.

Emperor gazes towards me “See…”

"What see, even I can do that" I said.

Emperor Akbar smiles "Oh really... then take it". He handled me the royal dagger. "Show us".

I put forward his anxious hands "yeah, sure why not". I hold the knife in a professional manner as if I was a proficient player.

I toss the dagger in the air, and suddenly in the mid it burns out into sparkles, lighting whole of the hall. The sparkles were tumbling down gingerly like the stars were falling on the ground. The scene I have never seen before, simply wow......

"I can't believe... this, it's amazing" I exclaimed.

"It's just the beginning... We will make you voyage the entire world" said Alexander.

Bhagat Singh came near me and pinched me on my left arm "See... it's not a dream. Wake up boy, there is ample work for you".

CH-15

Master meets the dog

I don't knew what it was, but one thing was clear, I was sitting between the spirits of such famous personalities, whom no one had ever seen together, alive or dead. And the other thing that was exasperating me was why the hell I was there.

I was sweating like anything and was drinking water given to me after seeing my edginess.

While drinking water I asked "But what you need from me? Let me go".

Alexander the Great said "You have to listen us, you have no other choice".

"I am telling you that I can't help you in any way, it all..."

Emperor Akbar interrupts "What you think? You are sitting with us, in such circumstances, it's just a co-incidence?"

"What you mean by that?"

Queen Elizabeth said "You were given the assignment of this 'Old Fort' by your head, Mr. Mehta. Am I right?"

"Yes you are right but..." staggered "But how you know that?"

King Ashoka stated "Why not anyone else was sent for this assignment? Why not anyone else was given that apartment? Why only you"?

"How would I..." I asked.

King Ashoka interrupted "It was nothing else than our longing, we wanted you to come here, that's why you were given this job".

Mahatma Gandhi added "You use to visit here only during the daylight, that's why you couldn't see anything during the day because we are imperceptible during the day,

And we failed to bring you here in the night".

"Those happening in your dreams, and all that signals were to indicate you something". Mr. Einstein "But you were unsuccessful to investigate anything from which we could indicate you anything".

King Ashoka said "All thanks to your lack of concentration due to your affection for the opposite sex".

I asked "What you mean..."

Emperor Akbar interrupted "So you were brought here in this manner".

I asked anxiously "Why you always interrupt in between".

Emperor Akbar stated "Because I know what you going to say, and I am not at all interested in that".

"You knew about the 'Mystery of the missing door of the Old Fort'" said King Ashoka. "But you didn't know this thing that it was obscured underneath your house. The Missing door is the only reason for our existence in this Fort, if both the doors were closed then we couldn't cross the threshold of this Palace".

Mr. Einstein added "You lost your scooter today? I was the one, who stole that queer obsolete looking naive creature. And all this toil was just to keep your dog away from your house for some time".

"Then we had to take all of your possessions out of your house, so that you could notice the primordial mislaid door of 'The Old Fort' under it" Bhagat Singh said.

"I think you could have found a better way" I said.

Emperor Akbar said "Nothing in this whole humankind is better than our ideas".

King Ashoka stated "You were brought here in the night, and when the sun has strained, and anyone who takes almighty's name from his heart, can see us from his naked eyes!"

I asked "But for what you have done all this? I mean, why me... why have you called me?"

Mahatma Gandhi added "Listen, listen my child, many people love us, has given us space in their hearts, and still remember us till now. But... but I am very embarrassed to say that we couldn't stop some big blunders from happening, some such things could be shunned which we can't stop. We have done such big mistakes in our lifetime, which have turned to worse in the present time".

"You are a historian, you know history from every corner, from 'H' to 'Y', You know what it is and what it teaches" said Emperor Akbar.

Bhagat Singh stated "History teaches us to follow the success path of your ancestors and not to repeat their mistakes. But you have to do something beyond it, something that is never done yet by any person on this earth".

"What?" I got frightened.

"See... the world is suspecting another war, THE WORLD WAR III" King Alexander. But no one knows when, and how...... But we know".

Akbar said "If World War III happens, there would be two main reasons, availability of Nuclear Bomb, and the conflict between India and Pakistan".

"Atom bomb is such a weapon which can make any country to proudly participate in the war" said Bhagat Singh. "And if the war started with the atom bomb (stressing on each word) everything would get burned. The World would not be left for any wars in the future...... Destruction... Total LOSS... Human Race will come to end".

Queen Elizabeth said "There would be two groups, one with India... and one against it".

I was still confused and frightened "You are using such heavy words and if if...f......" I sighs. "I am a common man, I can't do anything please leave me, I.. I have to go".

Emperor Akbar blared "Sit... sit down".

"Okey okey, but what can I do, I mean what I have to do" I said.

"Just stop the problem from where it had emerged".

"I didn't get it".

Emperor Akbar said "The thing that is to occur, will definitely happen. But if that only thing, doesn't emerge, then what will happen? ... Nothing......" seeing my weird expressions "Okey, I will make it easy for you." He hold a glass of water and placed it facing me. "I kept this glass, and it's there in front of you...... So...... what if I haven't kept it here few seconds before?... It wouldn't be here at this point".

Bhagat Singh stated "Simply, Stop the invention of The Atom Bomb".

"And the second mission is to stop India-Pakistan partition" said Mahatma Gandhi.

"You have to go back in time" said King Ashoka.

"Hey, what is this. All of you are mad or making me one?" I asked.

Mr. Einstein told "Ok, so... Have you ever heard of a rumor, that it could be possible that Scientist Elbert Einstein had made a Time Machine? But never revealed anything about it?"

"Yes!"

"And it's a truth" he said.

Interrupting the narration, Mr. Einstein anxiously said "It's a...a.. lie, completely lie, I don't want to listen anything further, I am going..."

Amar holds his hand "wait for god sake".

"Leave me, you have crossed your limit".

"The story has something more for you, even I didn't believed it, and asked the spirits......

"How could it be possible?"

"Yes, I had made 'The Time Machine'" replied Mr. Einstein. "Devoted my whole life, my whole experience, my energy, my time, I invested everything I had. I even risked my life, by not telling the authorities, neither my friends, nor my family. I even tested it on my dog, I made him wear the voyage watch and sway him to sit in the machine, and as per my expectation, the machine worked and I was succeeded in sending him to the future. Yes it worked, I had done it before anyone could do or may be no one could reach near it till decades. But what I had done to myself, I had became so cold-blooded, that knowing this fact that my dog would not return, as dogs doesn't know how to operate the machines. He was with me for last 7 years, my only companion, and I used him for a covetous experiment. Then I realized that how a Time Machine can make any person so much famished for power.... Just imagine Amar, it could be even worse than we could ever dream".

Mr. Einstein interrupts the narration "Oh Jesus, you know everything..."

Amar smiles wittily and continues the narration "Then he revealed me that..."

Mr. Einstein "There is one more bolt from the blue, young man."

"Now what? I asked.

"Your pet is the only dog whom I had tested 70 years ago and now you are taking care of." My mouth remained wide open, and he added "Yes! Scott, your dog, was my friend".

"Oh my God"!

Mr. Einstein interrupts the narration "Oh my God! Tell me that you are not lying, where is he? I believe you. I will do whatever you will say. Where is he?"

"He would be......" Giving a thought Amar starts making perplexing faces "Oh no... Oh my God!" And he stands up.

"What happened?" Asks Sophie.

"He is in the car's boot" replies Amar.

"Oh no", the scientist cries out "he should had been died till now, my dog... my car. All because of you".

"Hey, see your car is alright".

And suddenly the car gets disengage from the branches of the tree and bumps onto the ground with a thummm......

"Oh my 'God'!" screams Amar.

"Oh my Dog!" Mr. Einstein runs towards the car, opens its boot, and gets flabbergasted to see his driver tied, with tape on the mouth and packed inside the diminutive boot. Scott jumps out from the drivers lap, starts revolving around the scientist and barks "Old man Old man......"

"My son"! Mr. Einstein takes him in the lap and runs his hand on his body. He raises his eyes and addresses Amar as an army chief orders his men. "Bring the driver out".

Amar opens the ropes that he had tied on driver's hands and legs, and helps him to come out of the car. The driver removes the tape that is on his mouth and starts breathing heavily. He holds Amar from his collar, "You......"

And he bangs his head hard on Amar's face. He kicks him hard on his abdomen, and Amar knocks down in the vicinity of the tyre of the car, a small bottle fells out from the inner pocket of his coat.

Scott jumps out from scientist's lap, ran towards the driver and barks "You bloody dog!"

He hops and bites the driver's butt with his prickly teeth, the driver starts screaming stridently. Amar manages to stand up and grasps the bottle lying on the ground. He is struggling to stand still and starts opening the cap of the bottle.

"No, not again!" The driver screams.

"Your only mistake is that you resemble my Boss" and Amar throws the bottle towards the driver and the liquid inside the bottle tips out on his face.

"I will not lea......" and the driver knocks down on the ground.

Amar points towards Scott and said "We both know how to use our weapons".

"What was that?" Raman.

Mr. Einstein holds Amar's collars "What have you done to my driver?"

"I never wanted to do that" he said while removing scientist's hands from his neck.

Sophie rushes to the site where the driver was plunged, she turns on her knees, took his face in her hands and asks, "Is he alive?"

"Yes he would be alright in just fifteen minutes" replies Amar.

"Are you sure?" the scientist ensures.

Amar gives a wage reply. "I don't know, but..."

Mr. Einstein asks fumingly "What do you mean by that?"

"I was just told the same".

Amar's replies hoists the level of scientist's rage "What?"

"Stop!!! stop stop..." Sophie interferes. "You both have started again, first draw the driver near the fire, it's so bitterly cold".

Amar holds the driver from his legs and starts dragging him towards the flame. Accompanying him Scott holding his pants from his teeth, starts imitating his master. The scientist holds the dog from his back. Scott was moving his feet as he was liking his job, the scientist takes him into his lap, pampers him by running his hands over his body, and the white creature answers him by licking his face, the scientist starts laughing and Scott too starts barking, illustrating that even he liked the reunion immeasurably.

CH-16

Stipulation for the Time Machine

Scott is trying to catch the ash that is flying from the fire, but the scientist, in whose lap he is sitting, is not letting him to move. Amar spreads his legs, kicks the driver lying beside to create some room. Confiscating his eyes from those of Sophie's, which are gaping him since so long.

Amar lowers his eyes and proceeds scratchily "Ahemmm...... It was kind of a miracle, I couldn't believe that I had a dog with me who was a part of such a life-size discovery. He gazes Scott and and a pinch of smile glows on his face. "I was unable to understand that how could it be possible? and..." and he continues the story.

Mr. Einstein was gazing into my eyes, he hold my hand and said "Your pet is the only dog whom I had tested 70 years ago and now you are taking care of. Yes! your dog, was my friend".

"Oh my God!" I was taken aback. "Is it possible?"

"Yes it is......" replied Queen Elizabeth-.

Bhagat Singh said "You have to believe us", and he smiled. "You don't have any choice".

"That I know" I said in a lower voice.

"Then put the foot on the paddle and proceed!" King Alexander said while raising his hand graciously.

"But what I have to do? I have a simple idea, leave me and I will find a person for you, who don't have any job".

"Hey you silly boy..." Emperor Akbar said furiously.

I literarily trembled "I was just joking, what I need to do?"

"It's an important part of history" said Mahatma Gandhi, "when in 1939 Scientist Elbert Einstein had signed a conformation letter to the, then President of The United States of America, Franklin Roosevelt, to give his avowal to draw on his research for any purpose according to needs of the nation and humanity. But contrary to his expectations, his research was misused to make Atom bomb, which was then bombarded in 1945".

"You have to go in the past, and manage to convince the scientist to not sign the letter" King Alexander said it in one go.

"And how could I do that?" I asked.

"Go to 'Google dot com' or do whatever" Emperor Akbar mocked, "it's all your headache. I don't understand one thing that if these sites can give people the technical information about how to make a bomb, then why they don't give any information to stop it".

"It's not fare, the dilemma is yours and you are putting the entire burden on me".

Emperor Akbar asked heatedly "Then?"

"Then... nothing......" I startled.

"Then... Mr. Einstein knows what to do" Queen Elizabeth looked at the scientist and smiled.

Mr. Einstein smiled back to her. "Don't see like that Your Highness. I know it's my turn". And he gave a droll look at me "I need your help young man".

I got mystified "For what?"

"We have to make a Time Machine". Before that my inquisitiveness could ask anything the he proclaimed among others, "I need some goods..."

"Ask the young man to arrange it..." said King Ashoka.

"But how?" I asked.

"Find out a buried treasure, loot a bank...... whatever, anything that can help... Bhagat Singh mocked.

"What?"

"You are the one...... Then suddenly the scientist stopped and started poundering something, "wait wait, we have your goods, that we have stolen from your house."

"What? My belongings? Are they here?"

"Will they help?" Mahatma Gandhi asked.

"They will......" replied the scientist.

"What are you saying, how could my bed, my fan help you to make a time machine?"

Mr. Einstein widened his eyes "Wait, and watch......"

Jampacked with excitement, Mr. Einstein interrupts the narration "I know what he is going to do" and he laughs......

"Who?" asks Sophie.

"I... the Ghost Einstein......"

"Wow..." Raman exclaims, "It looks like a fiction story, a fairy tale. Now I understand little bit. Superhero Amar at a super confidential mission to save the world...

wooo...... So you are like Fred Astaire types superhero? It's my pleasure that I have earned a friend like you today".

"Friend?" asks Amar.

"Yes......Really... you are a real hero Amar. I wish I was like you, my wife would have been so proud of me".

CH-17

The stranger goes back

It is 4 in the morning, and the policemen are unable to find the kidnapper and the scientist. They have made their fleeting base camp in the center of the forest. Some of the policemen are setting the tents and some are keeping the dead bodies of the co-policemen in the van who died during the car blast. And abruptly the jeep of Officer Clark arrives to the site. He swiftly applies brakes and jumps out of the police jeep. One of the policemen who are betrothed in setting the tents left his work and runs towards him.

Officer Clark walks hastily in one of the tents and addresses to the policeman "What's the progress?"

"Sir almost all of our men are back, and unfortunately they are without any information. Only officer Bhatt didn't turn up." Policeman follows him inside the tent and says timidly "I think sir, the scientist and that barmy kidnapper died in the car accident, and if they have survived, till now they would have been killed by the wild animals".

"Don't give too much hassle to your grey cells young man". He opens the map lying on the table, "Where has Officer Bhatt gone"?

"In the north Eastern part of the woods, Sir".

"They are alive".

"What?"

"Officer Bhatt has found them......"

At the other part of the woods, the six of them, scientist, Sophie, Amar, Raman, driver and Scott are present unknowingly that policemen are seeing the sights like ravenous dogs.

"I really appreciate your candor and truthfulness Amar" said Raman.

"What?" Amar replies while he notices that Sophie was smiling timidly.

"You were preferred because... because you are a good man... with a good heart".

Mr. Einstein added "No doubt he is".

"Really" Amar watches disclosure at the scientist, "Well... thanks".

All of a sudden Raman stands up.

"Where are you going?" Sophie asks him.

"Just to munch some fresh air. I will be back" and without uttering any other word, he leave the place.

Amar stands up "Do it fast, we need to go".

"Now where are we going"? Sophie asks the same question to him.

Mr. Einstein stands too "What happen?"

"He was a police informer" says Amar, "we need to leave this place as soon as possible. Police would be here anytime".

Sophie inquires "How could you be so sure?"

"Just do what I say" hewals towards the car. "Will your car work?"

"First budge the driver into the car" Mr. Einstein orders.

Amar rushes towards the driver and pulls him from his arms "Scott, go into the car". He throws the driver into the car and sits on the driver seat.

Sophie sits behind the driver's seat "Do you think it will start?"

"Of course it will..." Mr. Einstein added.

"I hope you are right." And Amar Folds his hands and watches upwards. "Oh God!" He moves his neck back." Just pray to god that it starts!" And he inserts the key and tries to start the engine.

Eeeeeehn... eeeeeehn......

Sophie folds her hands too "Please..."

Eeeeeehn... eeeeeehn......

Sitting at scientist's lap Scott barks "Lets go......"

Eeeeeehn...... eeehn... whooom... whoooooom... and unexpectedly the car starts, Amar puts the first gear and force down the accelerator and car moves leaving the tepid place.

CH-18

The spilled Coffee beans

The car has invaded deep inside the woods leaving the place they had resided far behind.

Sophie turns back and looks out from the filthy back glass of the car "I think we have came quiet far from that place." She turns back, sits straight, leans forward and keeps her right hand on Amar's shoulder, "I don't think that they can find us?"

"Then?" asks Mr. Einstein.

"Hmmm..." coming back from his reverie he continues "What?"

"What happened next, Amar?"

Amar takes a breath "Huh...... I had to leave the Palace that night, to prepare myself for the unsighted expedition. The Scientist assured me for giving me the Time machine till next night. I just knew one thing that 'I am going back in Time, to amend it, for a healthier future of the humankind'. These words felt simple when I first heard them from King Ashoka, but I didn't realize that what a life-size encumbers were on my shoulders. I took Scott along and spend the rest of darkness in the nearby church, watching continuously at a sculpture of Lord Jesus, recalling my encounter with one I found in the palace, just trying to find the answer for that one question that was revolving around my mind, 'WAS THAT GOD'?"

The next morning I took out my phone out of my pocket, but alas it was not working, the foolish gadget couldn't even bear a single encounter with the floorboards. I had to go near the central mall. I had no money so I asked for 5 cents from a passerby and straightly entered a telephone booth outside the mall with Scott. I dialed a no. on the dialing pad.

Tring tring...

"Hello..." I said into the receiver.

"Hello"

"Hello... Meghana... it's me".

"Amar? What do you want now?"

"Its really very urgent dear, I want to..."

Meghana interrupted “I don’t want to talk to you”.

“Listen I am in a big dilemma and I…”

She interrupted again “Don’t try to trap me in your emotional ambushes Amar, you never cared for me,” she started crying “never…”

“Let me…”

Yet again she interrupted “The way you talked to me last night, is it a way one …” she whimpered.

“Hey, please…” and I got distracted from a toddler banging the door of the telephone booth from outside.

The kid standing outside started shouting “Hey! Do it fast man!!!”

“Please stop crying, let me clear myself dear, last night I was…”

“Hurry up you dirty creature”, the kid started kicking the glass. “Come out!”

I showed a slap to the boy, Scott started barking at the boy after seeing that “Ssshhh… hello, Meghana…”

“I don’t want to talk. Bye…” and she disconnected the phone.

I removed the receiver from my ears and watched it “Really? She disconnects my call?”

The boy standing outside started kicking the door and making weird faces, I gnashed my teeth and kicked the glass with such a vigor, that it broke.

I started watching left and right to see if anyone had noticed me, and contradictory to my anticipation, a policeman started darting towards me. I jumped out of the booth and started running, unfamiliar to the fact that I was holding the receiver of the phone.

Scott screamed "Dad, phone!"

And when the wire got stretched, I was pulled with the strong force of the steel wire of the telephone and I shoddily fell on the ground along with the telephone machine which got detached with the glass back, breaking it into pieces. The policeman ran towards me hastily showing me the stick.

Policeman leaned towards me and hold my hands "Stand up you scoundrel".

Scott entered the sizzling site and "You bloody dog", and he bit on the policeman's butt.

Interrupting the narration Mr. Einstein says "That what I was wondering, he never did such things when he was with me, nor ever I had taught him anything like this. These all violence had been taught to him in your violent era".

Amar continues the narration "Scott was holding the policeman's butt with his spiky teeth, the policeman threw his stick and held Scott from his back and started whirling there due to extreme twinges. I managed to stand and ordered Scott."

"Scott! Leave him, let's go", and I started running at my acme speed, Scott grabbed a piece of his pants as one more achievement in his anthology and followed me, leaving the policeman lamenting due to agonizing pain and veiling his frayed pants.

I went straight to Meghana's house as the crow flies. I stood in front of the door but thought that it wouldn't be a good idea to ring the bell as she would not open the door on seeing me. I went across the hedges towards the backside of the house where I found the window of the kitchen wide open. I jumped to catch hold of the window so that I could enter in, but it was beyond my reach. Then my eyes caught on a grass mowing machine present nearby. Unknown to the fact that Meghana was in the kitchen, I kept machine under the window pane and tried to climb on it to reach to my destination. As I got hold of the ledge under the window, my foot stroked the switch of the machine which started moving with a jerk leaving me lean on the wall. Meghana came towards the window hearing the sound created by breaking of clay pots which were wrecked by the moving Grass Mowing Machine. The moment she was going to lean from the window to see what happened, I managed to climb up the window due to continuous shaking of my legs and uphill struggle. The sudden entry of her so called 'Ex-Boyfriend', (as she had decisive few minutes ago) petrified her so badly that she screamed appallingly throwing the bottle of the coffee, that she was holding in her hands.

Listening to her scream, a wavering voice of an aged woman came from inside the house. "Megha, what happened"?

Meghana replied stridently "Nothing Grandma......" Sitting on her knees and amassing the conked out pieces of the bottle, she addressed me in hushed voice "What are you doing here?" All of a sudden a piece of glass hit her finger. "Aa... a ouch!"

I saw blood coming out of her finger and held her hand charily. I took out the piece that was pricked in her finger. She clogged her eyes, and I put her finger in my mouth. She gingerly took her finger out......

I rolled my tongue around my lips "Ummm... your blood tangs like cappuccino!"

She smiled "It's because the coffee was stick to my hand while picking up the pieces" and she chuckled, "haha... ouch" she realized about the cut on her finger. "ssssss......"

"Go bring the band aid, I will tie on your finger".

"What happened to you last night?" she asked.

"It's a very protracted tale, dear. I am trapped in a big dilemma at this moment". I hold her hands" I need your help".

From the other room Meghana's Grandmother called "Megha!"

I siad “I need some money”.

Meghana’s Grandmother called her again “Megha! My coffee…”

“Meghana?” I asked her.

“Leave my hand, grandma is calling me”.

“You are my only hope, please help me out”.

“If you didn’t need the money, then you would had never came here to meet me. Am I right?”

“No, it’s not true, I really…”

“Yes, it is. Amar, you are so mean”.

Abruptly we realized that her grandmother was standing in front of us, gawping at both of us.

Grandmother asked “Why are you both fighting”?

I threw away her hand “Nothing a…ummm… grandma”.

“I just came to take my coff…” Grandmother watched the broken bottle of coffee on the floor. “Oh no”. She leaned to clear it off.

“I…I will do it Grandma, you go” said Meghana. “I am bringing the coffee for you”.

"First come in my room, I need to talk to you" and grandmother left the kitchen.

She gathered the broken pieces and threw them in the dustbin, "You always create a problem for me, Amar" Meghana said to me in a very hushed tone.

Grandmother called from the other room "Megha!"

Meghana stared at me "Coming Grandma". And she left me alone in the kitchen and entered her grandmother's room. Cleaning her hands from the apron that she was wearing, she asked her grandmother, "Yes Grandma".

In a very inquisitive and teasing manner grandmother asked "Who is he?"

Meghana replied bashfully "He is my friend".

"Do you like him?"

She pressed her lips with her teeth "ummm... grandma..."

Grandmother interrupted "He looks good, but does he wear such grubby clothes daily?" On realizing that I was trying to listen by standing near the door, she called me inside "Hey, you 'Mickey Mouse', come in here".

I scratched my head and congregated some valor to face the old lady and finally put forth my step to enter the room.

"What you want" she asked.

I went close to her "Grandma... my.. my name is Amar, and I am M..M...Me...Me..."

"I know you are her friend, but I asked what you want".

I bent on my knees and hold her feet "I am in a problem grandma, I have lost everything. I just wanted to meet your daughter and tell her that I still haven't lost the hope and trying to stand up again. I am ready for the game that the almighty has planned for me. But I need her help, I need some money".

"How much?"

Meghana interrupted "Grandma wait!"

"Quiet" Grandmother turned towards me "how much you need?"

After a minute of silence I stated "5000 Euros......"

Grandmother turned towards her bed, lifted her cushion and took out the keys beneath it. She went towards her cabinet and opened it with trembling hands. She opened the locker in it and took out a jute bag from it. "I have only 2150 Euros, I will give you the rest tomorrow, after withdrawing it from the bank".

"May be I wouldn't be in the city tomorrow" I replied.

"Where are you going?" asked Meghana.

Grandmother gave me the jute bag "Take it..."

Holding the bag in my hands I gazed it "I will return back the money when I will come back".

"Sure!" she said.

Meghana screamed "I am asking, where are you going?"

"Going to a voyage, but I promise I will come back soon". While watching towards Meghana I bid them a good bye "Thanks grandma, will miss you".

And I left the room and listened that Scott was barking from the backyard. I went straight to the kitchen.

"Where is he going?" Grandmother came out of the room and watched me climbing out of kitchen's window and screamed "Hey, we have a door too in our house." She turned towards Meghana and asked "Is this guy mad?..."

I jumped out and saw Scott trying to climb up the wall to see the bitch in the next house.

"Come on Scott, We have lot of work to do".

Scott turned his neck and scuttled towards me "I didn't do anything, she was saying that she liked my tail!"

We came out of Meghana's house, having what we needed... 'Money'. It sounds gluttonous, but...... I needed that. Without bringing to a halt we instantaneously went to the old French Souk.

We both were passing through that busy swarming market, and Scott was pulling my legs because he was continuously being hit by the passersby. I picked him up in my lap.

I hold a passerby by his arm "Do you know where is Ali?"

"That aaa... that dealer of the antique goods?" the passerby asked.

"Yes!"

He directed me by pointing his finger towards the end of the street "There, next to the hotdog stall".

I lifted my ankles to see through the crowd "Thanks!"

And I moved towards the shop, but was interrupted when a man suddenly held my hand.

He gingerly slanted my right hand and stared at my watch "It would be more than 50 years old". He lifted his eyes and stared me, "Want to sell it?"

I crouched my left eye and dragged my hand away "No..."

The stranger stood from the chair "Brother, what price you want?"

"I don't want to sell it..."

"Ok as you wish" He pointed towards the hotdog stall, "that's my shop, next to that snack stall. Come to me when your heart feels like selling it..."

"What's your name?' I asked.

"Ali... The whole market knows me"

"That's your shop? You are Ali?"

"See..." he smiled. "You were finding for me, and we met before Allah's premeditated encounter. What you want?"

I leaned and came close to his ears, "1930's Britain Pounds... worth Two thousand one hundred fifty Euros......"

I saw that exterior part of his left ear was damaged.

He got stunned "That's a big amount. I need some time, give me the money and come when the sun drowns".

I took out that jute bag out of his pocket and gave it to him "I will come at 5 in the evening".

"Now all your worries are mine, Insha Allah you will get what you want......"

I left the place, Scott was still in my lap licking my face, I turned his face away with my hands. Ali was seeing me till I was indiscernible in the crowd. He took out his phone from his left pocket, dialed a number and placed the phone near his ear.

"Hello sir..." He said while straightening his back.

"Hello" the receiver spoke.

"I have news for you" he said, "something that will make your soul blissful... He came to me..."

The man from the other side asked "Who?"

"Amar......"

CH-19

The officer and the scientist's car

The night has gone meek, the skies' tint is changing as if someone is adding milk to it. The moon is clearly visible, the blue is clear after so many days of drizzling showers. The Scientist's car is going through the wildest part of the woods, and is heading towards the urban side. On the other side, Raman has moved more profound inside the woods. He is cutting the bushes with his knife to clear the shaggy path, and is holding a torch in the other hand. He sees some movement through dense bushes, he has reached near the Police base. He soars out of the shrubberies and enters directly to Officer Clark's Tent. He lifts the curtain and goes inside the tent.

Raman pat his foot and salutes the Officer, "Officer Raman Bhatt reporting, sir".

“So Mr. Bhatt” Officer Clark is loading his weapons “What’s their location?”

“Whose?”

“The Kidnapper’s?” Officer Clark asks.

“I don’t know…”

Officer Clark fumes up “What do you mean by you don’t know?”

Officer Bhatt stresses at every word “Officer, It means that I don’t know”.

“Then what the hell were you doing the whole night in the woods”.

Officer Bhatt stares into the officer’s eyes with rage “I was doing my job Officer, It’s not my fault that I didn’t found them”.

Officer Clark throwing the riffle that he was holding and goes close to Officer Bhatt “So… you didn’t found anything?”

Officer Bhatt puts forth a step closer to him “No… I haven’t Officer……”

“So, you want me to believe you?”

Officer Bhatt keeps a finger on his chest “Do whatever you feel like……” and creates stillness at the place.

Officer Clark breaks the silence "You can leave officer......"

Officer Bhatt comes out of the tent and starts revolving his prying eyes all over the place, he sees a jeep and stride towards it. He sits inside it and drives it out of the scene towards the city with a whooom....

Officer Clark was standing outside his tent and watching his jeep perturbing the reconciled dust. He runs inside the tent to get his revolver. He comes out of his tent and screams "Take out the jeep......"

A policeman runs towards the Officer listening to him screaming, "Yes sir?"

Officer Clark reloads his revolver "Take out the jeep, we need to go immediately".

"Yes sir."

The Policeman runs towards the jeep and drives it towards the Officer.

"Hasten up". The Officer puts inside his revolver and sits inside the jeep "Lets go......"

Unfamiliar of the proceeding at the foe, the scientist's car is heading towards the city.

Amar checks the meter "We are out of fuel".

"Can it help us in reaching to the Research Center?" the scientist asks.

"I don't know" he replies.

After giving a thought, Sophie asks "Why you needed that money?"

"To survive in your city..."

"So did you go back to Ali in the evening"? Mr. Einstein asks.

"Yes, after coming from his the market I went to the Morgue room of the city, to read the old newspapers of 1930's and 40's, so that I could gather more information. And I reached the market fifteen minutes before the planned meeting. I was waiting in his shop as he was not there. I was twisting the paper weight while sitting on the chair and Scott was lying on my boots, but swiftly stood up by listening to some conversation outside".

Speaking to the Hotdog vendor from outside the shop, Ali started blaring not knowing the fact that I was sitting inside, "Don't scream, I will return your cup".

He entered his shop holding a cup of coffee. But as he saw me, he threw his cup on the floor and started running deep within the crowd. I picked the paper weight in my hand and went out of the shop. I threw the paper weight at him, which hit him at his back. He collided with a passerby and fell on the ground. I jumped on him and gave him a punch. I pressed his neck "You scoundrel, you want to flee with my money, take this then", I hit him on his nose, Scott came running and started pulling his hairs with his jaws.

"W..wait... wait..." Ali cried "I don't have your money. I have given them... aaaaa..."

"Leave him Scott!" I commanded.

Scott leaves him "This kind of people doesn't understand like this".

"Now speak up you rascal..."

"A person said that, you have sent him" he disclosed, "I had given the English Currency to him".

"Who was he, and where has he gone"? I blared "Speak up".

"I don't know... I don't know......"

I left him "Huh..." I stood up, I was breathing heavily, "Come on Scott".

Scott barked at him "I know that you are lying"!

I had left with no way out, instead of going to the palace empty handed. It was getting dark and we had to promptly rush to the Palace. We both were running between the busy heavy traffic, jumping over the barricades, dashing between the crowds as the crow flies. We were running on the grubby lane of the Palace crunching the dried leaves. And when we crossed the threshold and came inside the Eerie Fort, I got flabbergasted to see my Scooter in the center of the hall. But it wasn't the like that, which it used to be before the time when it was stolen.

There were two big fans, one on the front where the headlight is supposed to be present, and another on the back of the chair which replaced the ordinary seat of the scooter. Big flashing head lights were fastened at the front, gigantic wings were attached on its base. A big operating gadget box was attached underneath the handle. Giant neon gas cylinders were affixed on its back, and the two-wheeler was glowingly illuminated all over with fastidious beams of lights.

I headed towards the machine in revelation "**Oh my God"**!

And somebody hit me with a vase on my head, I turned my neck and it was Munish. He kicked me and I fell on the floor. Scott ran towards him to save me, Munish threw the vase, picked up a chair.

"You bloody Dog!" and Scott jumped towards Munish.

Munish turned around and strike Scott hard with the chair. Scott fell along with the chair on the contiguous wall. He started crying like anything, and Munish started chortling. I stood up and held him with his collar. He kicked me on my stomach and I knocked out down on the floor.

I lifted up my head and screamed "You have got your Egypt assignment, what else you want".

He took out the jute bag which I had given to Ali "1930's English Pounds, worth Two thousand one hundred fifty Euros……" he showed it to me "Is it yours?"

I was lying on the floor, I screamed "Give it back you Bastard..."

"Not now Mickey Mouse... first tell me why you need it".

I tried to stand up "None of your business..."

"Why are you here? And what's that behind you?" He pointed towards my scooter. "What are your plans Amar?" He blared "Tell me... I can't afford to lose my position at this level, you don't know what all I had done for all this, and I can't let everything go like this." He screamed in ear-piercingly "What are you up to Amar?" And he pushed me away with enormous vigor.

I fell on my scooter behind me and my hand socked in its handle, and automatically my watch got affixed to a rotund bend on the knob. Out of the blue, all the lights of the machine started glowing and the immense encompassing fans started revolving. Munish got timid and started moving back. The fans started moving so promptly that it felt like clashing of blustery winds of a storm. The floor was wavering, and I started pulling away my hand but it was struck in that curved bend.

I blared "Aaaaa!..."

And suddenly my watch opened from its strap and I fell back due to continuous force applied by me against the machine. It was strange for me as the watch was opened for the first time I had worn it. I was watching at my wrist when the bewildered baddie picked up the vase again and ran towards me. I grasp his hand which he had lifted to hit me, I twisted it towards his back and hit him on his face with my forehead. The vase skipped from his hands and he stepped back. I gyrated my vision to locate the chair with which he had hit Scott. I picked the chair and smashed it hard on him, he fell on the ground and got unconscious. I ran towards him.

I leaned and slapped on his face "Hey! ... Hey Munish...... '**OH MY GOD'**! What has happened to him? Hey listen, I didn't want to kill you...... Are you listening?

Somebody held me from my shoulders and I turned back with bewilderment. And I found Mahatma Gandhi standing in front of me, with the rest of the people sitting on the large table, with the chandelier glittering and the candles on the candlesticks burning.

"I..."

Mahatma Gandhi patted my shoulders "He is alright..."

"I was just... I didn't want to hurt him..."

Bhagat Singh stood and headed towards me "You didn't do anything wrong. You were just defending yourself". He went near Munish and took him in his arms "He just didn't know what he was up to". And he made him sit at a corner of a wall "In fact I am very contented, that you have started fighting for yourself, and against the wrong".

"You have to be brave Amar" Emperor Akbar added. "You are going for a 'Big Battle'."

"But I don't know, how he had this information that I will come in the palace"? I asked them.

"Take it as your ordeal", said King Ashoka, "And you have come out from it with triumph, and shown to all of us that you are the one, whom we were discovering since decades".

"And moreover, that gadget had also chosen you" Mr. Einstein stated, "as it was appended on your wrist so long. This only watch will direct you where to go".

I pointed towards the queer looking scooter "And what you have done to this"?

"It's your Time Machine......"

I gazed the Machine thoroughly, it was glittering in the dark "Wow! ......"

"It's time for you to go... But listen one thing, I have presented you 'The Time Machine', only because we rely on you and feel that you will not shatter our expectations".

I nodded my head "Never!"

When you will attach your watch with the machine, you will be transported to the time and place, which you will set on it. But there are some limitations that you will have to follow". He gave a pause, stared into my eyes and continues. "The Time machine will work only for some limited time so that after your missions are accomplished, no one could exploit it".

"It means that you have to complete your work and have to return promptly after that......" Queen Elizabeth added.

Interrupting the narration Sophie asks "So you will go back?"

"I have to..."

Jampacked with inquisitiveness Mr. Einstein asks "Then..."

Amar proceeds "I had to leave that place...... Bhagat Singh came to me and hugged me".

And everyone followed him and made a circle around me. It felt like a profound relation was established with them within few countable hours of gloom. I put forth my step and touched Emperor Akbar's feet. He grins and put his hand in the pocket of his royal kurta and took out a Knife belonging to the Mughal era.

He gave me the knife "Take my blessing along" and he kissed my forehead.

Then I went to King Alexander, he gave me a regal blue bottle "Its Roman camphene, it makes a person comatose. It's my yearning that its necessitation never arises". And he smiles.

I walked towards Bhagat Singh and leaned to take his blessings. He simply removed his hat and placed it on my head. "Use the weapons in the way they should be use, and only then, when the weapon itself says to play it". And he handed over me his revolver too. "Mark my words, 'Disguise at the time of any life-size predicament'."

"But there is a condition my son" said Mahatma Gandhi. "You will not go violent, and promise me that there would be no loss of life... I gift you the weapon of non violence". I touched his feet and he pated my back.

"Now go and take your dog along..." Scientist commanded.

I lifted Scott in my arms, he was trembling due to immense pain in his leg.

"You have to do one more work for me".

"What"?

Mr. Einstein pointed towards Scott "Leave this poor creature from where he had come".

"But why?"

Mahatma Gandhi added "It's considered good, if the body which had given up his soul get merge into the soil where it had arrived from".

Mr. Einstein notices my gloomy face "Respect the time young man, you should leave now. All the best, meet you there in the past".

I sat on the machine, put my hand on the gadget and it got locked without my intervention. As told by the scientist I set the time and the place where I had to go......

Sophie Interrupts the narration "Then?"

"Nothing, it didn't started..." replies Amar.

Mr. Einstein gets amazed "Oh my God!"

"I also said the same... 'Oh My God'...... And the machine started heading ahead, the main door of the palace opened on its own and my scooter picked up a speed that it had never reached till date. It came out of the palace, and gingerly started lifting from the ground, and at last it started flying......"

"Then?" asks Sophie.

"After that I couldn't see anything...... Whooom... whooom...... whoooooom... flaaaaaash and at last ... Thaa"

She asks the peak of prying "Then?"

"Then what, unluckily I was here. And the rest you know..." He takes a deep breath "I didn't know what will happen, I didn't know that you will believe me or not, I don't even know this thing that when I will return, I would be breathing or not...

Mr. Einstein keeps hand on his shoulder "I am with you Amar..."

Sophie follows "I am also with you…"

Scott barks "I am always with you…"

"Thanks guys!"

All of a sudden a bullet is fire that hit the tyre of the car.
Thaa…

Amar watches at the rear view mirror "Oh my God, a police jeep is chasing us".

Sophie gets alarmed "No".

The car starts vacillating, so Amar taked his head out to see the tires. The left tyre of the flipside has burst out. Then he tries to see who was driving the jeep, and as per his expectations, Officer Clark is sitting in it along with one more policeman. Officer Clark takes his revolver out and shoots three more bullets.
Thaa Thaa Thaa...

The bullet crosses with dreadfully less gap near Amar's left ear.

Amar turns his head towards Einstein "What to do now…"

"See, there is a giant obstacle in front of us. I have left the Letter signed at the Office. And according to me, police would have confined the whole edifice till now. There would be tight security there.

In Officer's jeep Officer Clark asks the policeman "What I told you, wasn't I right? Now see, what I will do". And he points his gun to shoot at his aim.

Thaa......

The rear glass of the car brakes into pieces.

"Aaaaa......" Sophie Huggs Scott and coves him with her hands.

"You have to go there and destroy the Letter at any cost" says Mr. Einstein.

Thaa Thaa...

"See you have to go, so that anyone else couldn't get hold of it".

While driving vigilantly Amar replies "But how?"

"Jump..."

Thaa... The officer shoots the tail light..

"What?" aska Amar.

"I said you leave the steering, I will see".

Amar opens the door of the car and leaps out. Following him Scott also hops out of the car. Einstein sits on the driving seat and holds the steering in his hands. Amar and Scott escapes in the darkness of the woods and in the reverberations of continuous firing.

Thaa Thaa...

"Run Scott run......"

Scott barks "What the hell is going on?"

Officer Clark is incessantly firing from his jeep.
Thaa Thaa Thaa...
And one bullet hits the other tyre. The tyre bursts out and the car starts vacillating very shoddily.

Mr. Einstein gets startled "Oh no!"

The car goes out of control and gets struck into a tree. Officer applies an earsplitting brake producing screeching noise. He reloads his gun and swiftly leaps out of his jeep with the policeman. Pointing the gun towards the car, he warily opens the door of the car. He finds the Scientist sitting at the driver seat and Sophie at the back with the driver lying unconscious.

Officer points the gun towards the driver "Who is he, and where that scandalous criminal has gone?"

Mr. Einstein revolves the steering of the stagnant car mischievously "He is my driver. He got tired that's why he is sleeping". Sophie passes a fake grin, and thw scientist continues, “We are on a night Safari, and I am driving the......”

Officer Clark interrupts by bashing his hand stiffly on the car’s roof, and yelled “I asked, where is he?”

Sophie gets terrified “We don’t know... we don’t know...”

“If you know that he was here, then find him” replies the scientist.

Officer Clark bellows “I will...”

Mr. Einstein interrupts him and counter attacks “You don’t know me officer. Behave properly or I will make you repent on your words...”

Officer Clark reacts in resentment “Huh......” he turns around and holds his head, and kicks the tyre twice” No no... “He raises his wrist near to his eyes to see his watch properly in the dark. He addresses his policeman “Don’t worry... The sun is going to arise......”

CH-20

The camouflage

Amar and Scott are scuttling continuously since one hour but manage to reach near the city before the crack of the dawn.

Scott spots the road and the board of the post office, which is visible from the bushes, "See dad, we have reached the city!"

"I know Scott that you are parched as we are running since so long. The thirst for water is perturbing me too. Wait..." He starts finding for water "See there it is" he points at a water tap. "Come on Scott..."

They lope towards the tap and Amar leans on the tap to douse his drought. And as he stands straight, he gets dumbfounded to see his poster on the wall above the tap, declaring shoot at sight orders, and asserting heavy reward for the one who will give his information, with 'WANTED INDIAN TERRORIST' written in bold letters.

"Oh my God!"

"Dad gone famous!" And Scott pulls his pants and points him towards his back "Dad, see at your back!"

"What?" And he turns back "Oh no!"

All the walls, all the lampposts...... his posters are affixed everywhere with the same Wanted tag.

"This is the same photograph that was clicked in the lock up. Oh no! What to......" He stops by listening to the sound of tapping of boots, he addresses Scott in lower voice "Shhhh...... follow me". He left the tap running and both of them veiled behind the bushes.

Busy in their conversations, two policeman arrive towards the spot.

"You tell me, what could I do in that case? It's like finding for the target in the murk". The fat policeman says to the other.

"Completely agree with you..." replies the one with the big golden mustache.

"Disguise at the time of any life-size predicament", Amar murmurs in his mouth. "Bhagat ji, I remember, what you taught me. And I even know how to bring it into play. Thank you!"

"When is your next appointment with the psychiatrist? You really need it" Scott barks while seeing his master talking to himself.

"Shhhh..." Amar scolds him.

Coming across Amar's poster, the obese policeman points towards it "What a bastard, the only reason for our standing in the frosty night, away from our wife and our sleep.

Amar throws a stone far-off breaking glass of the shop

Crash!

Turning his neck the fat policeman asks "What happened there?"

"You stay, I will see..." and the other policeman darts towards the place from where the crashing sound emerged.

"Call me if there is any problem..."

Amar whispers in Scott's ear "You have to do me a favor Scott".

"Really, once again" Scott smiles.

The Policeman watches the tap running "People are so careless". He goes near the tap to close it.

Amar pats him flippantly on his back "Go!"

Scott leaps out of the bushes "You bloody dog!" and he hops and grabs his butt in his sturdy teeth. The policeman shrieks deafeningly.

Amar emerges out of the bushes, wedges his mouth by his hand, and lugs him into the bushes.

The other policeman arrives scuttling and start finding his comrade. "Roger... Roger...... He goes ahead in the lane "Where has he gone?" And he goes out of the sight.

Amar exposes his head out of the bushes and starts seeing in all the directions. "Come on Scott!"

They both circumspectly come out of the hedgy bushes. Startlingly Amar is now wearing the Police uniform which he has removed from that policeman who is lying stripped behind the shrubberies.

"Why you have removed his clothes? Whatever, but you are looking damn cute!"

Amar takes a deep breath "huuuhhh...... Scott... Are you game?"

"Yes dad!"

"Then let's go!"

CH-21

The letter's battle

The sun has started diffusing into the blue. Amar and Scott are heading towards The Science and Research center's building. The road is looking busier than what it seemed the previous day. Lots of cars, police jeeps, and ample of crowd are covering almost every inch of the area. Ample of barricades are installed to stop the civilians and journalists to enter the place. The building is copiously captured by the police force. According to the authorities, the stranger had kidnapped the scientist from that treacherous place, that's why they are evacuating the building and are investigating the whole vicinity, to get some evidence that may possibly help them in locating the Indian terrorist. And the super sturdy security illustrates the blazed pressure which is laid by the higher authorities. The investigation is on its peak.

"I didn't expect this much". On reaching the hot spot Amar sees the policemen stopping the journalists to enter from the main gate. "I think we have to find another way Scott".

And he heads towards the adjacent wall, thinking as if he would climb it unobtrusively.

A Police Officer notices him going towards the flipside. He follows him and...

Seeing Amar keeping his foot on the dustbin, the officer asks "What are you doing?"

Amar anxiously takes of his foot on the spur of the moment, and starts thumping his pants as if he was cleaning his trousers and not trying to climb the wall.

"Go and load the chemicals" the Officer orders.

Amar and Scott both start watching back to see to whom the officer was addressing.

"I am talking to you, take these keys". Amar takes out his hand perplexingly "This one is of the jeep and this one is of the store room. He hands over him the keys and points him towards a police jeep on the road. "There, that jeep... drive it inside..."

Amar interrupts "From the main gate?"

'Yes from the main gate. And load the chemicals in the store room in the jeep".

"Okay... oh! Yes Sir!"

"Be watchful, the chemicals are flammable!"

"Flammable!!! Okay, very good... I mean Yes Sir, I will.. I will......"

"I will meet you in within 5 minutes".

Amar nods his head and runs towards the jeep.

"Come in Scott we have got the ticket to see the action!" Amar says.

Scott manages to hop inside the jeep which is loftier than his capacity. Amar starts the engine and press the accelerator.

"Lets go!"

Seeing the crowd in front of the gate Scott barks "Get aside get aside... my car is coming my car is coming yeah!!! Get aside......"

The mob slice into two pieces, to let the jeep go through. Amar drives the car from the main gate, the policemen at the gate salutes him, and he also greets them back with a smirk. He parks his jeep inside, near the police cars and vans and strides out.

After watching ample of policemen inside the center's premises Scott states "Hey Dad! All of you are wearing the same uniform, it looks like a school assembly. Isn't it?"

Amar sees a police driver loading goods in the adjacent van. He goes near him and... "Where is the store room?"

The driver lifts his eyes, and starts pondering something but didn't replied.

Amar repeated while stressing on each word "Where is the 'Store room'???"

"Have we ever met each other before?"

Amar starts sliding his face gingerly, and manages his tilted police cap. "No!"

"I think I have......" He stops for a pause and finally breaks the silence "The store room is there". He points him towards a door.

"Thanks". And he goes towards the store room.

"Where had I seen him?" The driver starts thinking something "...... Oh no!"

At the other side, Amar has opened the lock and is picking the boxes containing the chemicals. 'Danger, Flammable material', the big warning in bold letters itself depicts the danger that it can cause. Amar takes them out of the room in a trolley and keeps them inside his jeep. He returns inside the room and out of the blue he sees that driver standing in front of him.

"Now I remember who are you?" and the driver hits Amar on his face, throwing away his cap. Then he holds him from his shoulder "So, let's go back home Mr. Terrorist..."

And suddenly the police jeep, which is brought by Amar, explodes with a BANG!

Driver sees the car blazing "Oh no!"

Amar kicks him hard at his abdominal part and throws him back", Got your answer, that who I am?

The adjacent police cars and the vans also catch fire and blew up in the sky.

Amar comes out of the room and screams "Scott..."

Scott lopes in the picture and stands in front of him.

"Go and cut the water pipe... Go!!......"

All the policemen gather at the sizzling spot around the burning police vehicles.

A Policeman screams "Bring the fire extinguishers and call the Fire brigade... Hurry up!"

There is a condition of hue and cry among the policemen. Everyone one is running here and there. And between so many policemen, an adorable little white dog is running amid their legs. He is finding for the sleek long hideous thing, which is ordered to be destroyed. He sees the pipe rolled around a copper holder attached with wall. He hops on the pipe and starts gnawing it.

At the other side, Officer Bhatt enters the main gate in his jeep. He comes out swiftly seeing the scene of the burning cars.

Officer Bhatt asks the driver who was smacked up by Amar "Hey! Come here... What happened?"

"Sir, the terrorist is inside the building's premises. He attacked me and set the cars on fire. All of the chemicals have been destroyed and the fire is spreading very rapidly".

Giving a thought Officer Bhatt replies "You go and bring the water pipe first, I will cater with him." He presses his teeth in anger "Run... fast!"

The driver runs to take the water pipe and to opens the water outlet, but gets astonished to see Scott sitting on the pieces of the pipe, holding on in his mouth. The obedient pet of that historian has finished his job perfectly.

"You bastard!" says Police driver.

He leans to catch the uncultured creature, but Scott jumps and holds his nose. Driver starts blaring out of pain, but Scott wasn't ready to leave him. Listening to the cry, Officer Bhatt arrives to the spot. "I told you to..." watching the extravaganza "Oh! So you are here".

Scott leaves the driver's nose and letting him blubber out of pain "From where you got this uniform silly hunter?"

"Where is your master?"

Scott hunkers down his eyes "You think that I am going to tell you?" And he escapes from between his legs.

Officer Bhatt runs behind him to chase him. At the other side, Amar is cutting down the electricity wires and the telephone wires in the Electricity room. Scott enters the room hastily, with his long tongue hanging out.

"So... Officer, Is the job done?" asks Amar.

"Yes sir!"

"I hope that someone hasn't noticed you entering here. Wait, let me first close the door".

Amar goes to the door and as he locks it and turns back, someone starts banging it from outside.

"I know that you are in, open the door!" Officer Bhatt bangs from outside.

"Oh no! Scott, come..."

Amar jumps the window opens to the other side and Scott does the same. "Scott, see... I have to go upstairs in the office. You have to take care of these policemen, can you do it?"

"Yes! I will!" Scott barks.

"All the best!"

"Same to you, Dad!"

Scott scuttles outside where the policemen and Officers are throwing water on the burning cars. The injured driver is standing in the middle of the ground and suddenly notices Scott running.

Police Driver indignantly yells to other fellow policemen "Hey see, that is the dog of the terrorist. Catch the dog, the terrorist is here and the dog may have the suicidal bomb".

Everyone gets alert, after listening about the bomb. All the Policemen, start lifting their sleeves to get ready for the chase……

Then what…

Scott is running ahead, and group of policemen and officers chasing him behind. The cute little creature is hopping from one bench to other, is skating under the cars, and policemen are banging with the poles, falling in the pits and are slipping on the floor. It seems like a difficult chase for the world renowned skilled English Policemen.

And till then Amar manages to climb the sewage pipe to reach to the window of the scientist's office, which he had broken last night by making a smashing entry. He cautiously enters the room from the broken window pane. The room is like the same, messy, bullet spots everywhere, on the wall, chairs, doors, like the same that he had left last night. Taking his eye out of the surroundings, he starts finding for the letter.

And outside, in the ground of the center premises, it is a scene which has glued the eyes of the public and is entertaining the passersby for quite some time. Scott is jumping from one place to other, from one window to other, and making the policeman struck in the window panes. It can be easily seen that the dog is proving heavier on dozens of policemen.

And in all this clamors and ciaos, Amar is finding for the scientist's letter. He is lifting the files, checking the drawers, inspecting the cupboards... He hasn't left any stone unturned...

Amar smashes the files on the table in antagonism "Where is the letter?" And suddenly something falls on the ground. "What is it?" He crouches his eyes and leans to pick it up, that was a folded paper. He opened it and... "The letter, the signed letter, I got it... Yes!"

And suddenly the door opens with a bang and one policeman is standing before him.

"Hands up..."

"Oh my God!" he puts the letter in his left pocket and raises both his hands.

Policeman says "Hey Daniel! Come here, I have caught him". He turns to Amar, "take out that page that you have just put in your pocket..." The other policeman enters the room and he also points his loaded gun towards him. "Come on, take that out..."

"Hey listen!" Amar tries to clear.

The Policeman fires near his left foot "Keep it on the table!"

Amar takes out the letter and puts it on the table. And suddenly Officer Bhatt enters the room.

Officer Bhatt addressed the policemen "So... you have arrested him? I would recommend you for the promotions and the gallantry awards".

"Thank you sir!"

Officer Bhatt orders "Now leave..."

"Sir?" the policeman asks.

"Don't worry" Officer Bhatt takes out his revolver "I am here. Go and arrange a police van to take him to the police station".

"Sir, should I inform the head quarters?"

"Aaa... No... Do what I have told you" Officer Bhatt says.

"Yes sir" and both the policemen left the room.

"So... I was right" says Amar "You are a police officer..."

"Yes......"

"You called me your friend... You all policemen are the same..."

"Put your hands down gentleman......" says Officer Bhatt "I could have easily got you arrested last night... In fact you should be thankful to me..."

Amar descends his hands "Oh..." he says in rage "so it's like that..."

Officer Bhatt keeps his hands on his shoulder "Listen Amar...... I ... am with you... Just do what I say... come with me......"

Amar removes his hands from his shoulder "You mean that you are here to help me?" He Raising his eyebrows "Don't think that I am a fool..."

"Amar... Please don't misread me. Trust me... You have to trust me..." he throws his gun towards his feet "Please... Do what I am saying. I know for what cause you are doing it. I believe in you, so please believe in me. I remember that I said that I am your friend, and I mean that......"

Amar lowers eyes depicts that he have started believing in him "Where is the scientist and Sophie?"

"They are alright and in police custody for the inquiry. Police is suspecting Sophie to be involved with you".

"Oh no...... Poor girl..."

"Now come on, follow me. Hurry up". Officer Bhatt smirks. "Or otherwise I will shoot yo..."

Thaa...

And out of the blue a bullet fires and Bhatt falls on the floor. Amar runs towards him and took his head in his lap. The bullet was fired on his head from the back. Amar lifts his eyes and saw Officer Clark standing in front of him, with a loaded gun in one hand, and Scott in the other.

He has hold Scott viciously from his neck, and Scott was whimpering agonizingly.

Officer Clark continues “Caught you!” Amar stands and as he is going to put forth his step towards him, he points his gun towards him “Get back...”

“Why have you killed him?”

Officer Clark presses his teeth “Because I knew that he is of no use to me”. and he fastens his grip on Scott’s neck in resentment, and Scott screams out of tremendous pain.

Amar bellows “Leave him you bastard!”

Officer Clark laughs to see Amar getting agitated “Hahaha... I know, till I have a hold on your dog, I have a hold on you...”

Abruptly Amar takes out a revolver out of his coat and shoots Scott.

Thaa......

Clark gets terrified and throws the dead Scott away in bewilderment. Lifeless Scott falls on the floor, with his tongue out of his mouth.

Amar speaks confidently “Now......”

“You can’t do this...” Officer Clark holds his collar “You can’t do this bastard......”

“Definitely, I can...”

And he punchs him hard in his stomach, and hits him hard on his face. The revolver falls from his hands, and he sees blood coming out of his nose, he pushs him and throws him on the fallen chairs. He heads towards him, but Amar kicks him and Officer Clark too falls on the floor. Amar stands up and hops on the table to grasp the letter. Officer Clark manages to stand properly and hit him on his back, Amar turns back and Officer Clark make him lean on the table and holds a pen from the pen stands and tries to hit Amar with it. Amar holds him with his arm and... ....

Amar shouts "Scott!!!!!! ......"

The stunned Clark turns his neck and sees the dead creature standing and shaking his body to come in action, he is dashing towards him and then he elevated his forward legs and soars in the air... He is heading towards him like a bullet... Clark knows what was going to happen...

And it happens......

Scott is holding his but in his brawny jaws and the Officer is screaming like anything. Amar takes out the royal blue bottle out of his coat and throws the liquid towards the officer.

"Oh...no......" and Officer Clark goes unconscious and bangs on the floor.

Amar says to Scott "Scott, leave him..."

"No..." says Scott "He is a dog... Bastard..."

"Leave him I said".

Scott does the same.

"We need to go..." Amar watches down from the window.

And he sees that more force was called, as his presence in the building was assured. Fire Brigade, Press, Special Police Force, Army... All are standing for his reception. And he also knows this thing, that if he goes downstairs... There would be more no. of bullets in his body, than the no. of bones it has...

"Scott..." calls Amar. "We need to tie the officer with the chair".

Scott Yawns "Yaaaa...aa ... Okay..."

Amar holds the letter and stares at it "We have to do something..."

"What?"

"Lets go!"

CH - 22

The Final Chapter

The crowd is increasing as if it is a fare. All the policemen are standing downstairs in the shooting position, in front of the door. So that, wherever the disguised terrorist who is wearing the police uniforms, is seen in the area, he can be killed.

And suddenly someone is seen descending the stairs. The policemen lift their riffles and gets ready to shoot. And it is observed that two people in police uniform and one dog are descending down. And he is none other than Amar, dragging Officer Bhatt towards outside. All the policemen gets staggered.

Policeman Sees Amar dragging the unconscious Officer and screams "Sir!!"

Amar points the gun towards the policeman "Hey! Back... move back... Or I will sho... shoot the Officer". He keeps the gun under Officer Bhatt's chin.

None of the policemen or the army Officer knows that Officer Bhatt is dead. Amar has covered his face with his hand, and the cap on his head is hiding the bleeding wound of the bullet shot. And everyone is also unfamiliar with the fact that the gun that he is pointing towards everyone, is the same gun that was gifted to him by the young revolutionist 'Bhagat Singh', and from which he had shot Scott. And hence the gun contains fake bullets. All the policemen gets aside giving him the way. Amar is heading audaciously towards the main gate.

Amar goes near the police car, and addresses the policeman standing near it "Give me the key of the car..." The bewildered policeman starts watching here and there "Do it fast, my fingers will not wait for you, I can press the trigger anytime... Fast!!"

The policeman lamentably took out the keys from his pocket and throws it towards Amar. He manages it to catch from his left hand and opens the door of the car. He makes the Officer's body sit on the front seat. Scott jumps inside from the opened window. The policeman comes near the car to get a glimpse of the Officer. Amar points the gun towards everyone and sits in the car. He starts the car and rushes it out of the crowd.

Whoooooom......

All the people who are gazing the scene since so long are stunned to see how a one lean simple looking guy took the Officer along and escaped from the hands of the

Police Force and the Army... The car goes far from the vision of the helpless crowd, standing at the main gate of the 'Science and Research Center'.

Amar turns his face back to see if anyone was chasing them. But the road is empty as that they have covered quite a distance to assure their safety for some time now.

They are safe...
"We have done it!" barks Scott.

Amar sees blood slipping out of Bhatt's forehead. He picks a piece of cloth kept on the bonnet of the car, and wipes it off. His eyes get drenched, and he starts sobbing. He is broken... badly...

He knows that Bhatt had helped him altruistically at every step... sacrificed his life and now, his dead body brought him out of the lion's den......

He takes out the letter and tears it off to terminate his mission. And he throws the pieces of the paper at Bhatt's feet, to give the real hero, a tribute......

Now the mission is not only about him... It includes Bhatt's Martyrdom for humanity... Einstein's fidelity... And Sophie's love for Amar......

'Amar' is a Hindi word, which means one who is immortal. And the young Indian guy has justified his name. The ordinary looking guy has created History... Whenever Einstein would be remembered, or anything would be written on him, this incidence would come into sight every time, that how a guy kidnapped the World famous Scientist, and shook whole of the Britain and the rest of the World.

Amar has changed the past for a better future. He has done an out of reach job, which no one would have ever even dreamed about. But...... The work has not completed yet. Now he needs to go back to his time to get himself prepared for the next mission.

As the car moves on and on...... till it goes out of the sight... It is believed that the History will Rewind once again... One more Time Machine will be invented... With one more encounter with 'The Eminent Souls'......

The End